# STONE COLD MAGE

JAMIE HAWKE

ELDER TREE PRESS

STONE COLD MAGE is a work of fiction.

All of the characters, organizations, and events portrayed in this novel are either products of the author's imagination or are used fictitiously. Sometimes both.

# WELCOME

Want to never miss one of my releases and exclusive promotions? Sign up for my VIP mailing list:
**SIGN UP HERE**

Plus you'll get a **free** copy of my novel EX SUCCUBUS when you join.

**Want to be part of my FB group?**

*WARNING: This book contains gratuitous violence and sex.*
It's a group for readers to come together and share their

lives, passion for books, discuss the series, and speak directly with me, the author. Please check it out and join when you get the chance!

Thank you for taking a chance on my books. I hope you love reading them as much as I loved writing them!

Jamie Hawke

# 1

I had always envied my aunt in her large house atop a hill, until the day I had to move into it. Leaving my old life behind, my friends, Steph, all of it… fucking sucked. We'd only ever driven by it when staying in D.C., on our way to the cheapest hotels we could find on the southeast side. That had been enough of a taste to tell me I wanted more.

While I was starting school in the fall at Johns Hopkins University, my family didn't have the money to put me up anywhere in the meantime. Well, when I say my family, I mean my parents, because apparently my aunt was loaded. But that didn't translate over to my mom and dad, who were on the far side of the spectrum. I mean it—I still remember days spent in the rain of Portland, Oregon, wearing trash bags with holes cut out as we asked for money to catch the bus home. It fucking sucked. So I would look at pictures of Aunt Gertrude's house and remember the times we'd driven past it the one time we'd gone to D.C. for my dad's new job—the one that allowed us to move from our ratty apartment to our first townhouse—the way I had asked my parents why we couldn't stay there, and how they had avoided the question.

Not even invited over once, and their excuse was that Aunt Gertrude liked to keep her place clean, not liking little kids. It wasn't until much later that I learned she and my mother had both been in love with my father, and that they'd essentially sworn off their relationship.

So it was that I'd never even met her until that hot, muggy day of summer three months before school was supposed to start. Three months, because my father had apparently lost the job he'd come out here to get, so my parents decided they'd be taking that road trip around the U.S. they'd always been talking about.

Essentially, they were homeless and didn't know what to do with me. There I was, dropped off outside this huge mansion, and staring up at the tall, arched windows with pillars on either side. And at the top, leaning out over the edge and staring down at me… were those gargoyles. I had to laugh, wondering who the fuck built houses with gargoyles. Even more, who bought them? There was no doubt, my aunt wasn't only crazy rich, she was stupid rich. Why that was and where she got her money was a question neither of my parents could answer, and was something I meant to get to the bottom of during my stay. I was determined to be more like her, less like my parents —in the good sense, anyway.

Hell, even the air smelled richer out here. Pure, like someone had taken bottles of air from some tropical island and dumped them all over this neighborhood. For all I knew, that might've happened.

My phone buzzed and I pulled it out to see an image of Steph's breasts, her text reading: *Hop on and show me yours when you get into your room. I can't be there, but we still have to christen it.*

I frowned, glancing back to see my parents still in the car. They waved at me, and I waved back. My text in reply to Steph said: *No way am I jacking off my first day in the new house. Especially not on camera. Sorry.*

All that got was a sad face emoji, followed by the image of her tits vanishing. *Not fair,* I thought, not even knowing that you could delete images you sent. *Maybe if I could figure it out, I'd send that dick pic she wanted,* I thought with a chuckle. The pressure in my pants made standing there awkward, so I had to adjust myself and try not to think about the blowjob she'd given me that morning in her room before I left. Of course, trying to block out the memory made it worse.

I walked up to this huge house, overwhelmed by the curving wrought-iron fence, the white columns leading up to a patio above, and the black lantern hanging in front of the curved doorway. Statues of lions guarded the door on each side, and I had to pause to appreciate their intricate design. No, not lions exactly, I realized. These were the Okinawan ones I had learned about during a trip to a botanical garden that had a section devoted to the islands. Kind of like a lion mixed with dog, one with its mouth open, the other shut. I couldn't recall all the details, but knew these *shisa* were meant to be wards that protected from evils.

The door opened without me even ringing the bell, revealing a woman in a black dress with her silver hair done up in a bun.

"Aunt—" I started, only to be interrupted as she cleared her throat.

"Your aunt is out, but will return this evening," the woman said. "I help out around the house, and will show you to your room. Dinner will be left out for you, and I'll be on my way."

"Oh, okay. Thank you, Mrs…?"

"You can call me Fatiha."

I glanced back to where my parents' car had been, sighed as I wondered what I was getting myself into, and entered. The inside of the house was even more extravagant than the outside, if that was possible. There was a crisscrossed marble floor, pillars next to a grand staircase lined with deep red carpet, chandeliers hanging from the ceilings, and even candelabras on ledges throughout. The main entryway led off to a sunken living room on one side, while the other led to a dark room where I could barely make out a grand piano. It was as if someone wanted to rub my face in the fact that I had been so poor my whole life.

Rage built up inside my gut, causing my lip to twitch and my hands to ball into fists. How could my mom's sister live like this, while we had to struggle to survive? The idea that anyone in the world lived like this while so many struggled from one paycheck to the next and had to worry about rent checks clearing bothered me.

"Are you feeling well?" Fatiha asked, and I realized she was already most of the way up the stairs.

"Yes, sorry. Coming." I snatched at the handle of my suitcase and did my best to catch up.

At the top of the stairs I realized that there was another staircase farther back, but we didn't go to that one. Instead, we took a hall to the left that led to my room. After a pleasant, "Enjoy your stay," Fatiha was off.

There I was in this strange house, all by myself. My room looked like how a rich person thought a young man without as much money would have their room decorated, reminding me of something from the Disney channel. It was still twice as nice as any room I had ever slept in, and almost as big as the house I grew up in. The whole house. I set my suitcase next to the four-poster bed, stared at the white fireplace, and shook my head.

The heater turned on, a distant roar that rumbled through the underbelly of the house. Creaks set me on edge. For all I knew, the sounds could be people walking about. I went to the window, watching as Fatiha exited, and frowned. It might have been smart of me to ask if anyone else was in the house, although her earlier statements had led me to believe this wasn't the case. Still, the sounds of this old place weren't the type I enjoyed in a situation like this.

Fortunately, I had my parents stop at a falafel cart on the way, so I wasn't hungry. Otherwise I would have made straight for the dining room to at least have food to occupy my time. Instead, I saw that my room had its own bathroom, so I quickly took a shower. That would help calm the nerves, at least. But it wasn't enough, so when I stepped out, I leaned against the sink, closed my eyes, and focused. In my mind, I envisioned my nerves as a ball of unraveled string within me, but took that ball and brought it together, forced it to be one, to melt until it was a power source I could pull from.

It worked. But, before you give me any grief about visualization or meditation or whatever you might think of it, I have to tell you something about me—this was what made me special. We'll get into it later but suffice it to say, I wasn't like everyone else, even back then. And at the moment, I turned to a tried-and-true way of pulling myself together when I most needed to.

Looking up at myself, I saw this young, confident guy I knew I should always be. Others often told me I reminded them of Marty McFly from *Back to the Future,* but I was taller and I liked to think a bit buffer than Marty. Still, I got the resemblance and sometimes played it up, such as with the red jacket I had in the other room. My outfit of choice was basically jeans, a white T-shirt, and the red jacket. I shook out my brown hair so it had that messy 'I don't care' look and tossed my towel over the side of the shower.

I had just pulled on my pants when my phone rang. I was glad to see Steph's name on the screen.

"Fuck, it's good to hear your voice," I said, answering the phone after quickly throwing on a clean shirt from my suitcase.

"Took long enough," she replied. "All settled in?"

"If… that's even possible."

She chuckled. "How about that show, hmm?"

"Steph, it's not going to happen." Lowering my voice to make it clear, I added, "I'm not videoing myself jacking off. Sorry."

She laughed now, and I thought I heard it echoing from outside the phone as well. Frowning, I looked around, and then saw her there, standing outside.

"What… the… fuck." I went to the glass, staring at her there, perched on the branch outside my second-floor window.

"Thought you could give me the show in person. Maybe I'd get involved."

I still hadn't processed what was going on, but when she mimicked opening the window, I got the hint. Hanging up, I quickly opened it, but still didn't think to move out of the way to let her in.

"Steph, what're you doing here?"

"You don't get it, yet? I knew I'd miss you. Knew you weren't going to send me what I wanted…" Her eyes darted to my crotch, playfully. "So I hopped on the first plane I could find the moment you left. So… what'ya say?"

"Fuck."

"Fuck?" She scowled. "I fly all the way from Oregon to make sure your first night in this creepy place is amazing, and all you can say is 'fuck?'"

"I mean, you're amazing. Damn. I mean…" I finally stepped back, motioning her in.

"You're inviting me?" she asked.

The question caused a pain in my chest and a chill up my spine, my eyes moving for the door. My aunt had been kind enough to let me stay, and I didn't want to betray her trust on my first night. Still… this was Steph. What was I going to do, turn her away? My little friend downstairs certainly didn't want that.

"Just for a bit," I hissed, motioning her in. "If my aunt comes back and finds you…"

"Wait, she's not even here? Oh, that's rich. And what, she'll kick you out?" Steph climbed in, and only in the light was I able to see the cute outfit she had on. Black leggings or long socks, I don't know what they're called, which went up to her mid thighs and left a few inches of bare skin below her black skirt. A peppered brown sweater, her black hair coming down on her left side, wavy, and a tan beanie that didn't make sense in this humidity. She noticed my gaze and hit me. "Stop staring."

"Just... trying a new style?"

"Maybe I am. Like it?" She gave a spin, making it clear that my answer was a resounding yes. I fucking loved it.

At my nod, she bit her lip, pushed me back to the bed, and then straddled me. "What should we do?"

"I can think of a thing or two."

Her hands ran across my chest, moving down to my abs, and then she arched an eyebrow, looking at the door. "Let's see this place first."

"What?" I practically hissed.

"Come on, I've never been in a house this big. And... you said so yourself, she's not around, right? She's out. So... treat a girl." When she saw that I wasn't convinced, she leaned down, hand going between our bodies to caress my package. She whispered in my ear, "Maybe we find a special balcony to fuck on while looking out over the city. Hmm? Bend me over the railing, test my ability to not scream your name?"

"In the short amount of time since I left, you must've watched a lot of porn or something to get you this worked up."

She squeezed, playfully.

"Okay, okay," I said, unable to get the image out of my head of me doing her while the city lights sparkled beneath us. Seeing as I had no idea what my aunt would do if she found out I had a girl in the house, I figured it could be worth it. Maybe. At most, she'd probably give me a warning, since it would be my first—and likely last—time.

Steph giggled and ran off. Halfway up the next set of stairs, she turned, one foot three steps past the other, and looked back. At my angle, I didn't have a clear view of anything but saw a lot of leg. That was enough.

"Come here, you little tease," I growled playfully, and took off after her. She let out a giggle and ran off again until I caught her on the next level up, the two of us kissing, until I fell back and hit my head on the edge of a painting's oversized frame.

"Damn," I said, turning to see my aunt staring down at me. A painting of my aunt, that is. I actually recognized her, which surprised me since it had been so long. Pictures, I guess.

"That's her, huh?" Steph stepped up to the image, running a finger along the edge of the woman's white coat. "Fancy, like the house."

"Apparently," I replied, rubbing my head.

She turned back to me, pouted, and took my hand. "Come on, let's see if she has some frozen peas or something to put on that. Besides, I'm starved."

"That reminds me, there's food already made. I was hoping we could... build up an appetite first?"

Steph grinned, winked, and said, "Let's get you that ice, though."

"I'm fine, really."

She hesitated, glanced around, and nodded to a nearby door. My gut said to not go snooping. I hadn't even had a chance to say hello, and already I was going into rooms I wasn't sure it was okay for me to be in? But watching Steph's hips as she led the way, I didn't feel the choice was really mine.

It was dark in the room, and as soon as we were in, she

dropped my hand in order to walk up to a case full of old relics, staring in awe. Or not, as her eyes were darting across each item as if looking for something.

"What—" I started to ask, but she cut me off with a curse.

"All this, it's... I mean, how much can all this be worth?"

"Steph..." I cocked my head, hoping she wasn't going to suggest that we steal it and sell my aunt's possessions to make some money.

Her wink told me she wasn't going in that direction. "Only pondering. Don't be so uptight."

"I'm not uptight."

"Yeah?" She walked to the corner, looking over more glass cabinets with shelf upon shelf covered with items. Strange ones like ceramic dolls and little crystal figurines such as dragons and cats. One case was all plates with images painted on them. Steph turned to me, eyes full of mischief. "If she has all this junk out here, what do you suppose she has hidden?"

"Stop." I walked over to her, took her hands, and tried to kiss her.

She moved her lips aside and nibbled on my ear instead before saying, "Come on, let's see what we can find."

Going past me to cross the hall and enter the next room over, she started to make me worry. I hadn't known this girl long, and as far as I knew, she could be a total klepto.

"Steph, stop," I called out, then jogged after her, careful to shut the door behind me.

"I'm just having fun," she said, already looking around

the room, hands even tracing the wall as if looking for secret passages. "Have you ever been in a house like this? It's a first for me."

"Same."

"Well, live a little. Let the child in you come out and play—it's not like I really expect to find a closet of skeletons in here, but who knows, maybe she has a secret staircase that leads to a billiard room or something fun?"

"You want billiards, or you want to get some food?" I tried. "I thought you were hungry."

She scrunched her nose. "Billiards."

At that, apparently done with this room now, she moved on, brushing right past me. It was starting to get annoying, but I followed, realizing that the ball was in her court. I could get angry, tell her it was time to leave, but then she would be all kinds of pissed at me. Trying to seduce her clearly wasn't going to work, and I'd played the food angle.

Following her as she went through a couple more rooms, then down another set of stairs toward what I thought must be the kitchen area, I racked my brain for options here. When nothing came up, I said fuck it.

"Steph, this is it." We'd now arrived in what looked like the dining room, complete with a crystal chandelier gracing the ceiling. I looked around, sighing. "No more."

She turned to me with a smug smile. "That so?"

"Yes."

"Putting your foot down."

"I am."

"Fine." She stepped closer, letting one shoulder of her sweater fall and licking her lips. Slowly, eyes on mine, she got to her knees. "But… I've never given head under a chandelier before. Think of it as… mistletoe for the rich."

Was I so weak that this would dissuade me? I gulped as she nuzzled my crotch, and then breathed deep as she undid my belt first and then slowly unzipped my pants with her eyes still on mine. Yes, I was that weak.

It got even worse, though, when I heard a car come to a halt outside. Doors opening, then closing. Not even looking away, though, Steph had my firmly erect cock out and ran it along her cheek, down to her chin, then up to brush against her lip.

"You sure we can't just… try?" She moved it across her upper lip, then kissed the tip. "Real fast?"

What does a man say in that situation? Not a damn thing. A brief head nod, and I hoped to God my aunt would go straight to her study, or at least take her time getting into the house. I hadn't heard any doors closing yet.

"Make it fast."

She arched an eyebrow, chuckled, and ran her tongue in a circle around the head, before putting it in her mouth. With a pause, she said, "After this, we explore more. Pretend she's the enemy, and if she finds us—"

I grabbed her by the hair and shoved her down on my cock, feeling like an ass but also not interested in more talk of betraying my aunt's trust. Not right now. Shit, already the thought of it was making me start to lose my boner. The feeling of Steph moving up and down on it, apparently liking my forcefulness, took care of that real fast.

That is, until a door creaked open from an inner

walkway above. I cringed, hoping it wouldn't be my aunt, that she wouldn't look at least, but no such luck.

"Get rid of her," my aunt said, coldly, and I spun to see her at the top of the staircase. She shook her head, eyes full of anger. Before I could get a word of apology in or even tuck myself away, she had gone.

"Fuck."

"I can go," Steph said. But she yanked on my dick, pulling me toward her. "Or… finish you off."

"What?"

"I can't let my man get blue balls."

"Fuck, Steph. Come on." I pulled back, tucking it away. "This isn't right. I can't just… I mean, yeah… maybe go? I'll call you tomorrow."

She glared, not moving, so I just pointed back to the door I assumed was the exit, then ran after my aunt. "Let yourself out," I called over my shoulder as I went for the stairs.

# 2

"I'm sorry," I said, catching up with my aunt at the stairs as she was descending, going in the opposite direction.

She nodded, then motioned me to follow.

I did, without another word. Getting caught with my dick in a girl's mouth the first night after being invited to stay there made me look bad enough. The last thing I needed was to open my mouth and say something that would make me look even worse. There was no excuse for what I'd done.

She kept walking until we had reached a dark hallway with only one other door in it, at the very end.

Here, she paused. "How… No." She turned to me, eyes full of accusation. "How long have you known this girl?"

"She… moved to town—I mean, Portland—about a month ago. We've been dating ever since."

"Around the time I invited you to stay here."

"I—I guess." That certainly didn't make this sound better.

My aunt drew a deep breath, sighed, and looked like she was about to hit me. Instead, her hands moved around in a circle, a blue light showing. It hung there for a moment, then turned red.

"This isn't good," she said, eyes moving to me and dismissing the light.

Before the glow had cleared, or she had the chance to tell me what it meant, laughter filled the house. Not only Steph's laughter, although hers was definitely there, but I could also hear the shrill laughter of two others, at least, plus that of at least three men. As my nerves struck again, my aunt looked at me with horror.

"The girl… you let her in the house?"

"I… er, I don't know."

"DAMMIT!" She turned, hesitated, then faced me again in a fury. "You let her in… You!" Taking a breath to calm herself, she stared at me, eyes full of worry. "I never should've opened my door to you. You've doomed us all."

"That's… harsh," I said, but even as the words left my mouth, I knew there was much more going on here than I understood.

"Follow me, quickly," my aunt said, leading me to the door at the end of the hall.

"I don't understand," I started, and pulled out my cell. "Let me call the cops."

She held out a hand and a spark flew off my phone, the screen dying as smoke started to emerge from the sides and it grew incredibly hot. I dropped it, staring from the burning wreck of my phone to her glowing hand. She tucked it away, then turned toward the door, muttered something, and held the hand up. Again, it glowed, surging in brightness, and the door opened.

My mouth felt suddenly dry. "I really… don't… understand."

"This isn't simply a case of your girlfriend—soon to be ex, I hope—bringing her friends over to rob the place. Do you understand? This is…" She hung her head, grabbed me by the shirt and pulled me through the doorway. Once we were inside, the door closed. We were surrounded by pure darkness except for the glow of her hand.

She leaned close, voice hushed, "It's no coincidence, not at a time like this."

A candle lit behind her, on its own, then several more. She spun on her heel, went to a spot on the wall between two of the now-flickering candles, and pushed. It budged, then opened inward, revealing stairs on the other side.

Not even checking to see if I would follow, she marched up the stairs. Of course, I was right behind her. Each step was a reminder that I'd fucked up but also a reminder that I had no idea how, or to what extent, at least.

When I reached the top, I was out of breath and anxious, looking around a very well-lit room. Only, it wasn't natural light or electricity, it seemed, but some sort of glowing lights that were forming a square around us as my aunt chanted.

"Tell me," I said. Then louder, "What is going on?"

She paused, turned to me, and then went back to her chanting. A final glowing ball connected with the others, then lines shot through all, lines that separated and snaked out toward the walls. Now the walls and floors, everything, glowed green for a second before fading.

"A war," she grumbled. "The *shisa* outside would've

done their part, too, but I assume you invited the little bitch in."

"I... did." My instinct was to tell my aunt not to refer to the girl who had just been going down on me as a bitch, but in this case I was getting the impression that Steph had somehow royally fucked me over.

"Wonderful."

"What, like how a vampire needs inviting?" I scoffed. "Come on."

"It's similar, but in our case, demons, succubi, witches... all of that. I honestly don't know if any vampires are involved, but—"

"I'm sorry, go back. You're telling me you believe in demons and vampires?"

"And witches," she said, touching her finger to her nose. "Don't forget about them."

My mouth opened, then shut. Then finally opened again. Certainly there were words to reply to that, but they weren't coming to me right now.

"The thing you need to understand," she explained, "is that there's a whole world beneath the surface that you don't know the first thing about. Yes, demons, witches, all of that. Get over the shock, because it goes deeper—back to the days of elves, goblins... you name it."

"Bullshit." The word sort of slipped out without me realizing what I was saying. One sideways glance from her was all it took for me to say, "Sorry," and then she was motioning me to the closed door.

Before she opened it, she leaned in, lowering her voice. "I invited you for a reason, believe it or not. And you're going to have to put your big boy pants on for this, because we're not on the fucking bunny slopes."

Hearing my aunt swear, as poised and proper as she always seemed, hit me even harder than this talk of witches and elves.

"Why us?" was all I could think to say.

"You'll see, with time," she replied. "Right now, what I need you to understand is that you are so much more than you believe. So am I. We're going to work together, to bring back the world of magic. Are you with me?"

"If witches and whatnot are here, what do you mean by 'bring back,' exactly?"

Her eyes narrowed. "Remnants, only. Pieces of the puzzle left behind, those who fled. What I'm talking about, though, is a whole other le—"

Slamming doors and pops of explosions cut her off.

Laughter echoed all around, followed by a burst of light and what looked and sounded like shattering glass. It was the light from my aunt's ward, and as she saw it fall, her eyes filled with worry.

"We have to move, now!"

She had us moving through the doorway and running through a hall only to stop short as dark forms appeared, filling the opposite end of the passageway. They loomed and swayed unnaturally—and they were coming for us. Her hand had me by the forearm, grip unnaturally tight. She pulled me back and into a side room, then slammed the door shut behind us. Muttering to herself, her hand moved hypnotically, strange light trailing from her fingertips.

When a blue line formed in front of her, she turned to me. "Remember what I said." She grabbed me by the shoulders with both hands, staring into my eyes. For a moment, I thought she was going to kiss me—awkward, to say the least. "Don't forget, it's up to you."

She stumbled back, hit the wall, and looked up at the ceiling as the clattering of hooves sounded above. With clenched teeth and pushing through some pain that I couldn't understand, she reached for me with one hand, her other going to the wall beside her for balance.

The clattering grew louder. Darkness seeped into the room and filled it. Her blue line formed a spiderweb of lines around us, flickering like a bug-trap light when the shadows converged. They reached for me and were repelled, but suddenly changed tactics, all of them moving at once on a single point in the lines, bursting through, and entering my aunt through her chest.

She faced me with eyes that weren't scared, but determined. Her lips moved as if to say something, but instead of words, only thick, black blood emerged.

That same substance seemed to fill her eyes from within, and then she was on her knees, toppling over. A new glow came from her hand, this time starting to float over toward me in swirling blue tendrils. My hand reached out instinctively, and the light began to swirl, moving around my finger, then starting to enter me in a way that made my whole body tense up.

Getting back to what I'd done earlier to calm my nerves… there was a bit more to it. At the moment, I was searching for a way to calm myself. Knowing this was really happening but also conflicted because it had to be a hallucination, I searched my memory for ways I had dealt with similar situations, trying to think of any time I had tripped out like this. Nothing registered in that regard, but past experiences using my supposed power, or maybe magic, did come to mind.

For example, the time when I was ten, on a camping trip and some asshole in the next site over had been playing the most annoying trance music—I mean head splitting, kill-me-now crazy beats and synthesizer, whatever you call it. My whole family had been pissed, but me? I was on the verge of walking over there and punching this grown man in the nuts. Only, it didn't play out that way, because instead I was in the tent, hands over my ears rocking back and forth, my dad screaming at the man that he was going to murder him if he didn't turn off the music.

I'll go back a step, to when I was even younger, first. Hands over my ears while I rocked in the corner… had kinda been my thing. Call it whatever you want, but I don't ascribe to medical terms for my behavior, especially when I account for this next part. The fact that the day when the music had been bothering me, it suddenly changed to classical, then again to an upbeat jazz song that my dad had always played when trying to comfort me and get me out of my fits when I was young.

Having first assumed that was what was happening, I stopped rocking, stepped out of the tent, and looked around. Everyone was confused. My dad had a fist held back, one hand grabbing the man by his long, blue beard. Others were turning to look at me, curious. My mom knew that song, knew what it meant to me. Some of my cousins did, too.

And the strangest part? I was pretty sure I'd changed the music to that song. There was no other explanation—the guy insisted we'd done something weird to his phone where he'd been playing the music from, because no matter what song he selected, it would play that same jazz tune.

That hadn't been the only time. My dad and I had been going to grab a burger once, when I was about twelve. I remember not really wanting to go, because the wind was blowing like crazy and dark clouds were moving in. But we went, walking because the restaurant was close by. Right when we were within sight of the place, the rain came, but then it turned to hail.

We ran, and at first it was fun until my dad slipped and whacked his head on the curb. I started rocking… and then the hail was suddenly gone, warm sunshine on us. Only us. All around, the hail continued, but as my dad sat up, rubbing his head and looking at me, he knew something was off about the situation. And I knew I'd changed it all.

Call it a sort of alchemy of my surroundings. Not changing anything to gold, but changing the scenario, somehow. Always in simple ways, like the music and the sunshine.

So now, with my aunt dying there, floating lights swirling around her hands as she gasped for breath, I knew I needed to do something. To at least try. Even though my oddity had never worked like that—to heal someone, in this case—I knelt, rocking, hands to my ears. She continued to take those breaths, now sounding like sucking, grasping for life noises, and I rocked, not sure what to focus on here except for maybe the floating ribbons of light.

Only, a moment later she took a loud breath, then stopped altogether. The lights descended on her, and my panic took hold. If I lost her, I lost any semblance of sanity here. There had been magic, demonic forces at play, and without her I had no way of knowing what was going down.

The magic light was approaching, entering me. Burning. Pulling at my insides. Like a beast clawing to get out. Suddenly, I doubled over in pain and wondered how I was going to deal with this. How I could possibly escape this one.

Part of me said it was impossible, that this would be my end, as it had apparently been my aunt's. But another side of me said to fight, like all of the characters in my favorite games. Did they give up? When faced with the threat of not finding the third piece of the Triforce, had Link given up? No! And so I couldn't either. I had to live up to the legends of Simon Belmont, Master Chief, and the Mordor guy.

As these thoughts hit me, I realized something was happening. The light was changing, adapting to me and my thoughts. Just as the music had changed that day long ago, the light was forming a screen in front of me, words moving across the screen in a way that actually made sense.

The screen read: *You are being given these powers. Do you accept? Yes/No.*

I stared for a long moment, completely caught off-guard by this. My girlfriend and her friends had just killed my aunt. Now they were trying to kill me, as far as I knew, all to find something—I had no idea what. And, apparently, my aunt had some sort of power or magic that was becoming mine? Maybe I could've selected no, abandoned whatever this was and run off to join my parents on their road trip around America... but that sounded worse than anything a bunch of demons could throw at me. Sorry, but as I said, I had just moved out for the first time. That wasn't about to happen.

Plus, I already had something, whether it was powers or magic or whatever. My mom and the doctor had thought I was crazy, but part of me never accepted that. So, it's not like I was completely floored to find out that someone else in the family had powers as well. I clicked "Yes," and then watched as random runes scrolled across the screen, followed by: *Level 1 Witch.*

I frowned at that. Witch? Could a man be a witch? I scratched my head, trying to remember if Harry Potter had been called a witch or something else, but whatever. I could think of myself as a sorcerer or mage, if this was for real and anyone asked. *Oh, wizard! That's what he'd been called,* I thought, and laughed at myself for getting lost in such details, as I often did.

The idea of talking about whatever this was with someone made me freak out for a brief moment, until the screen changed again and pulled my attention back to it. Apparently, the screen was telling me my stats:

***Level 1 Witch***

***Statistics***
***Strength: 4***
***Defense: 4***
***Speed: 5***
***Luck: 7***
***Charisma: 6***

***Mana: 300***

***Current Spells***
***Passive: Situational Alchemy, AKA "Transmutation"***

THE BEST I COULD FIGURE, my sort of alchemist powers had converted the magic into a digestible format for my mind. Instead of simply taking on my aunt's magic, I'd converted it into a way of leveling up. Gamified it, you could say. While maybe she'd also started as a beginner and gotten stronger, been able to use more spells as she become more experienced, I would actually have a screen tracking my progress and telling me when I leveled up and all that.

Badass!

Maybe I'd call myself an Alchemist Witch, or something along those lines. I was starting to get into the idea, scrolling down the screen by touching it in mid-air although I couldn't feel it, exactly—it was more like using virtual reality controls, where it was clear when I was touching it, but there was no actual resistance—when an explosion sounded on the other side of the door.

Shit, I'd nearly forgotten about Steph and the demons. I was hoping my new powers would give me the ability to throw fire balls or something, but so far it looked pretty much useless, other than the stats on the screen making me feel a bit insecure about my strength. I had to be more than a four in that regard!

Another explosion, and smoke came through a crack

at the top of the wall. Now I heard their hooting and hollering. They weren't far from getting in, which meant I had to figure this out, *pronto*.

Whatever they were looking for, my aunt either had to have known about, or been searching for it as well. Right?

"Jericho, are you in there?" Steph said, and a new hope had been shattered—a hope that this was some fake version of the girl I had been dating. Most people called me Jay or simply J, and didn't even know my full name. She liked it, though, and preferred to use it, especially during sex. Her voice was smooth like caramel when she added, "I want you. Come on out."

All it took was a glance down at my aunt's corpse for me to shake my head and say, "Not a chance."

"Dammit, let us in or we'll fucking rip your head off!"

Shit, that escalated fast.

Another glance, and I shuddered, looking around for a way out. I tried using the magic, pulling up the screen again, but nothing worked. Figuring out how to use it would take time. A look back at my aunt, and I realized her hand was still out from when she had been reaching for the wall. Or… not reaching, but pointing!

I went to the wall, focused, and put up my hand. This time, while my hand didn't glow and open the wall magically, the screen returned. It showed an option for "open," so I selected it and waited.

Sure enough, my hand glowed and a door appeared. It opened inward, clunking my aunt in the head. I cringed, gently moved her out of the way as I whispered an apology, and then made my way up the steps.

# 3

This time, I was too freaked to bother caring about how far the stairs went or how exhausted I was. I pushed on, excitement starting to take over. As horrible as this situation was, I not only had magic, but it seemed I'd had some form of it all along. Being told you're crazy, or have a learning disability, only to find out it's not that at all, but a subtle form of magic? Brilliant.

Steph's voice came from below, more indistinct the farther I went, and then there was banging, smashing. Crashing.

I was at the end of the stairs, though, and found a wooden end to the staircase. Pushing up on it, I found that it opened up onto the roof. While I failed to see how this would be the safest place, there was no denying that my aunt had been telling me to go this way.

If not for the sounds of destruction below, this would have been the most beautiful, peaceful spot in the whole city. My aunt had the place decorated with a rooftop garden complete with a gazebo and gates covered in vines, and all of it looked out over D.C. On one side, I saw the National Cathedral, lit up in a way that made it look almost purple. A cold wind tousled my hair, making me wish that I had grabbed my jacket from my room.

A laugh escaped my lips as I considered how silly it was to be concerned over a jacket with everything else that was going on. Then again, what the hell really was happening? My girlfriend had turned out to be some sort of demon or something like that, she'd brought others like herself into my aunt's home, and killed my aunt?

The door slammed shut behind me. I jumped and took a few steps back, causing me to run into one of the vine-covered gates. I ducked around it, wanting to get away from that trap door before they came up after me, and spun around searching for ways down from here.

But, as I turned, I came face-to-face with a beautiful woman, mere inches away. Staggering back in confusion, I hit my head on the gate this time and cursed. When I looked again, I realized the woman was nothing more than a statue. A beautifully carved statue, but merely stone. And not exactly a woman, either, or not *just* a woman, I should say. The stone curved back from her head in what looked like four horns, under which were pointed ears. Her body was mostly on display, with what looked like stone armor and a loincloth covering key spots. She also had a spaded tail, along with great wings.

She was terrifying, and amazing.

So much so, that staring at this simple statue had almost made me forget the immediate threat. Banging on the hatch shook me from the moment, so I ducked behind the statue while hurriedly glancing around for options.

From what I could see, there were none.

That meant I could face a group of murderous demons—at best this being my delusional state taking over and they were simply regular, human murderers—or I could jump. I ran to the edge of the roof, glanced over, and decided that was the worst of the two options. While I wasn't too high up to survive the fall, I would likely break something. And then where would I be? Lying there, crippled, while Steph and her gang came after me. At least on the rooftop I could fight, and maybe my new powers would help me.

My hand reached as I grew dizzy. Heights had never been my thing. Feeling stone under my touch, I glanced over to see that my hand was on the shoulder of another one of these stone ladies. Gargoyles, I decided. This one was perched at the edge of the roof, looking out as if to defend the house from evil.

More banging on the hatch, and this time part of it splintered away.

I moved back away from the edge of the roof, back to the first gargoyle statue, figuring that if I stood behind her, at least they might try to attack the statue first, not realizing it wasn't real, leaving me with the opportunity for a sneak attack.

Another attack sent the hatch flying off its hinges. Go time.

Speaking of attacks, I needed to see if I had any options here. As holding up my hand had worked before, I did the same again here and found my screen floating in front of me, just off from the gargoyle's head. Maybe I didn't need to do it this way, and my aunt likely hadn't needed to, but the screen helped me process what was going on.

It listed several options, but others were blurred out, new screen options blurred as well. Meaning, there was room to grow, room to discover what I was capable of. If I lived long enough.

The one that caught my attention, though, as I leaned forward, other hand against the statue's wing, was an option that showed upon contact. It read, "Awaken."

My eyes shifted from the screen to the statue, narrowing as I wondered if this could be for real. Could I activate inanimate objects, like making a warrior of this statue? My own golem, in a sense?

"Jericho, it's time for the walls to come tumbling down," Steph called, knowing I hated that shit. For the first time since meeting her, the stupid saying actually kind of made sense.

A head appeared, looking about, not seeing me yet, luckily. I thought they would spot the screen, but apparently that was for my eyes only. The figure started to climb up to the rooftop, another behind, it, and I was able to see that these were not normal people. They wore red hoods with red, glowing eyes visible in the darkness beneath, and spiked armor that looked like it had come straight out of a Medieval Times show, the sort that would only be worn by the villains. Each carried swords that had small skulls on the hilts, adding to the name that came to mind for them: death knights.

Steph emerged after the first two death knights, and she had changed. Her hair was now white, her eyes glowing red. I don't know when she had time to put on another outfit, but she wore a black and red dress that went well with the death knights. Her hand sparked as she looked around, then an orange fire erupted, and her eyes locked on mine.

Shit. I didn't hesitate any longer, selecting 'Awaken' from my screen, and cringing as I waited to see what would happen. Nothing did.

"This is what it's come to?" Steph said, stepping toward me as more of her death knights followed, along with two others like her—a man and a woman, both looking older than her, maybe in their thirties. She paused, one arm crossed over her body, the other with hand up, fingers moving as she played with fire. "Give it to me, and we'll leave."

"Give…?" Maybe it should have come as a relief that I was suddenly much more confused than scared. "Is this some sort of sick, sexual game for you?"

"What?" Her eyes flashed bright and she growled. "Not—no, I don't mean your cock, you fucking pervert. Give me the Liahona!"

"I honestly have no idea what you're talking about." I stepped out of hiding, hands up to show her I wasn't a threat. "Call this off, go home. Maybe this is all a dream, I don't know, but it needs to stop."

"A dream?" She laughed. "A fucking dream? J, if this was a fucking dream, my mouth would still be around your cock. Do you see my mouth around your cock? No. So, wake the fuck up and tell me where it is!"

I wanted to say, 'in my pants,' as my response would've been to Steph any time before this strange experience. But, I knew she was referring to whatever strange object she was looking for, and I had no idea what that was or where it would be.

When I shook my head, she threw fire my way. A small ball of fire that surely would've taken out an eye or worse, had I not dodged back behind the statue. It hit stone, and there was a rumbling sound. The rooftop shook slightly, and Steph's team looked around in confusion.

She, however, hadn't broken her focus. "Tell me where to find the Liahona."

"What the fuck, Steph?" I shouted, scrambling back past the statue, behind another gate. "This isn't funny!"

"Do I look like I'm laughing?"

Hands snatched me up, the man who had been with her with his face inches from my own, and then we were moving through the shadows, him pinning me down in front of Steph. He was tall but wiry, with more pronounced cheekbones than looked natural, and a sickly yellow shade to his eyes.

"Best give her what she wants, boy," the man said, and then pulled back as Steph and the other woman—wiry hair and eyes of all black—leaned over me.

"Last chance." Steph pointed at me with long, red fingernails. Almost claws. The fire was moving between her fingers as if it had a life of its own. "Give me the Liahona, or die."

Another rumbling, this time enough to create a crack in the roof, and cause the wiry-haired woman to lose her footing and stumble back, falling on her ass. The death knights took up positions around Steph, and she turned, eyes narrowing.

For a few more seconds the rumbling continued, then all eyes turned, and I pushed myself up to see what had drawn their attention. There in the garden, the gargoyle statue I'd hidden behind glowed purple, light shining from cracks in the stone. The cracks spread and a heartbeat later the stone broke off, shooting out as the female beneath burst free, eyes glowing for a moment before the magic light faded and she was left standing there, glaring our way.

A beautiful, in the flesh, real-life gargoyle.

# 4

"What's the meaning of this?" the gargoyle asked in a soft, sensual voice. It was hard not to notice her barely-covered body, even as terror filled me. Her long, black, wavy hair fell over one shoulder. Her smooth skin had a slightly purple tint to it, and her horns and wings were red. Large breasts were held only by armor, the loincloth falling into place where it was needed below. She wore armor on her legs, forming at the feet into what looked almost like stilettos, but I imagined might have to do with a gargoyle's foot shape.

I kept telling myself that it had been me who woke her, so there was no reason to be afraid. But, that didn't stop the terror from seizing hold, even more so than when I saw Steph with her new magic and her retinue of death knights.

Instead of answering the gargoyle's question, Steph attacked with her fire. The flames around her hand shot out in three bursts. Her death knights raised their swords and moved forward as the gargoyle rolled out of the way of the first two shots. The third hit the backside of one of her wings, but only singed it lightly before dying out.

A growl escaped the gargoyle as she stood and thrust out a hand but… nothing happened. She seemed confused, then glanced back at her wings, seemingly equally confused, and let out a groan as the first death knight's sword came down on her. Suddenly, as if purely on instinct, the gargoyle became a fighting machine. She dodged the blade and came up with claws that tore into the man, tail whipping around to stab at his throat, wings flailing to catch a gust of wind and pull her back and out of the way of three more blasts.

The expression of anger and confusion on her face was priceless, and I almost felt bad for the death knights as she tucked her wings, diving back in to give them hell. Two vanished in puffs of smoke from her attacks, but the third managed to knock her back, sword raised. She spun, sweeping out his legs and snatching his sword, then plunged it into the knight's face, causing him and his sword to puff out of existence.

"What magic is this?" the man next to me demanded, staring wide-eyed at me.

"It doesn't make sense," Steph cut in, angered, as she threw another burst of fire. "The boy doesn't have this kind of power, and the searcher is dead."

Searcher? I assumed she meant my aunt but had no idea what was meant by the title. Then again, it seemed there was a whole lot I hadn't known about her.

"A mage in the mix?" the woman asked, pulling a wand from her cloak and turning, eyes darting about.

Meanwhile, the gargoyle managed to dodge around the death knight and pounced in our direction.

"Figure it out later," Steph said, moving her hand in a strange pattern and creating a shield of flames that caused the gargoyle to change her trajectory, going for the man instead of Steph.

The gargoyle plowed into him, lifting him, and while dark shadows began to pool around his hands, she threw him from the roof. Next, she was on the woman, who shouted words I didn't understand and flicked her wand, sending the gargoyle back with a black and green explosion.

A grunt, and the gargoyle was back at it, this time going for me. Both Steph and the witch watched this in confusion, neither moving as the gargoyle shouted in my face and attempted to swipe me with her claws. Only, she stopped with them an inch from my neck, sniffed me, and looked at me with curiosity.

"We're getting out of here," she said and rolled, grabbing me as she went, coming up on the other side and running with me held in her arms. Magic hit her and she almost stumbled. A death knight appeared a second later and nearly landed a blow on her, but then we were off, soaring through the air.

Not flying, I noticed, but gliding.

"The other one," I blurted out, realizing what was happening. "Your sister, or friend, or—"

"What?"

"She's back there, on the roof! They'll destroy her!"

The gargoyle looked at me in her arms, growled, and then adjusted course, flying back to land on a balcony one level below.

"You. Stay." She turned and leaped, claws digging into the side of the house, and started to climb back up to rejoin the fight. If we could wake the other one, I figured we had a shot at taking Steph and the others down.

Only problem was, I was apparently being left out of the fight.

"I have to come," I blurted out. "You need me to wake her."

She paused, glanced back, and asked, "It was you? You woke me?"

I nodded.

"Well then, great mage, hop on. I'll need you up there."

For some reason, I was smiling as I ran forward and jumped. Her tail hooked me under the arm and pulled me up so that I was on her back. The enemy hadn't realized that we had come back yet, apparently, because they were still shouting at each other about letting us get away.

There we were, climbing back into the thick of it like idiots.

"It's witch, actually," I mumbled.

"What?"

"I just… nothing." Thinking it over, 'mage' did sound cooler, even if my game screen said I was a witch. "Just, I'm only a level one mage, so…"

"Your words are gibberish."

"I mean, I'm not very powerful."

"But you woke me, meaning you're powerful enough. Worthy of saving Avalon, I'd wager."

As we reached the top, my mind spun with confusion over the words she'd just said, but the fact that we were about to charge back in against an enemy who seemed likely to kill me took precedence on my worry meter.

"What spells do you have?" she whispered.

I frowned, held up my hand, and looked over my screen. Aside from stats there was a passive skill called 'Searcher,' just like Steph and her friends had referred to my aunt, but otherwise, there was nothing.

"Stop that, you look like a fool." She glanced around, sticking low, wings folded against her back. "Tell me, what spells?"

"I'm checking," I hissed, trying to find out how to access other screens, hoping I was wrong. Giving in, I said, "Right now, none."

"That doesn't make sense. You said you were a mage."

"I… yes. But only level one. And I imagine I have to learn the spells, don't I?"

With a nod, she pursed her lips. "I can't believe you lived long enough to make it this far. How did you wake me?"

"I… touched you."

Her left eyebrow arched, the corner of her lip going up, but then the coldness returned as she gestured toward the edge of the roof. "Stay out of the way until we're ready. I'll charge over, distract them in battle, while you wake the other. Think you can handle that?"

"Yes." I projected confidence, in spite of the many deaths of me running through my mind. A fireball through the face, green magic turning me into a pile of dust, or whatever the hell that man was capable of, if the fall hadn't taken him out of the fight. Then there were the two or three remaining death knights and their swords. How could I forget about them, when the threat of my head being chopped off loomed over me?

To my horror, she was already slinking along the roof,

to the left of where I had first awoken her, leaving me with a clear shot for the other one. I did a quick scan to confirm it was the only other gargoyle statue up there, then crouched, legs ready to sprint.

A roar filled the night and she was on them—throwing a death knight from the roof and leaping to dig her claws into the witch. That was it, my chance. I sprinted all-out, making for the statue, and reached it as the gargoyle flew off the witch, taking a chunk of flesh with her. The witch was screaming, flinging hexes left and right without a target, and then I saw why—the gargoyle had not only torn flesh, but managed to scratch out her eyes. Damn.

Steph, meanwhile had her shield of fire again, shooting flames at the gargoyle while the last two of her death knights took up a defensive position. If they'd given up the offense, that meant we were looking good.

"Steph!" I shouted, reaching for the other gargoyle, smiling. "Let's see how well you hold up against two of them!"

My fingers touched the hand of the second gargoyle as Steph cursed and waved her hand to make her last two death knights vanish, then her. The witch was still there, moving her head about as she tried to work out what was happening, while the gargoyle was back up and preparing to pounce, but looking my way as I awoke the other.

I held up a hand for the screen as before. Only, this time the 'Awake' option wasn't there. In fact, it showed an image of a gargoyle in the upper right of the screen, along with what looked like a depleted mana bar.

What? I needed more magic, or more power, before I would be able to wake more gargoyles?

I grimaced and made eye contact with the first. Good

thing this hadn't happened before Steph left, or we might have been in trouble. As it was, the gargoyle growled, dodged an attack that came too close, and then ripped the witch's arms off before bashing her head into the concrete at the side of the rooftop. Finally, she took the witch's limp body and placed her against the side. With a swift strike from her tail, the spade was in the back of the head, severing something within, and then the gargoyle kicked. The head disconnected and fell over.

The body fell to the roof.

Turning to me, the gargoyle stomped over. "What's the problem?"

"Apparently, I'm not powerful enough to wake two, yet."

"Shit."

"I know. This… isn't good."

"The demon lady will be back." The gargoyle approached the other and crouched next to it to get a better look. "No, our situation isn't good at all, but it would be better if we had Kordelia on our team. This, by the way, is Kordelia."

"I see. And you are…?"

"Ebrill. And you?"

"Call me Jay. Short for Jericho, but I usually go by Jay."

She analyzed me for a second, then shook her head. "I'll call you Jericho. Has a nice ring to it. Does it mean anything?"

I frowned. "You're… joking, right? I mean, it's in the Bible, and…?" She was staring at me with a blank expression, so I shook my head. "Not important."

"At any rate, we should set up wards then get inside. You do at least know how to set up wards, I hope."

"Sorry."

She scrunched her nose, then motioned me over. "It's simple, really. Start like this," she held her hand up, then waved it across and in a semi-circle at the end, "curve it like this, and say, 'Ddiogelu.' Try it."

As she said the words, a blue line of light appeared in front of her, hovering there as if a flame had been dragged across and the image left behind captured on a camera. I nodded, figuring this was easy enough, and made the motion. "Dioglew."

"Again," she said, frowning. "Ddiogelu."

This time I said it right, "Ddiogelu," and the same light appeared. As it did, my screen flashed up and showed a new spell there, reading, *Barrier Ward: Ddiogelu.* It even showed a little motion that went along with the spell. Convenient, in case I forgot.

She saw me eyeing empty air—or so it appeared to her —and grunted. "Before, when you said you have no spells?"

"Ah, right." I turned, preparing to cast another, but she put a hand on my arm.

"Not necessary, but we should cover all four sides of the building, to be safe."

I nodded, walking with her to the next, as I explained, "I've always had this weird ability to sort of change things around me. Like once the air was all smoky at a campfire, so I sort of made it… not. Or when my buddy Devin was doing really badly in a PT test with me, wheezing and whatnot, I sort of touched his shoulder and gave him extra stamina and courage, I guess. It's all confusing, really. Maybe in my head, or—"

"You're a transmuter," she said, voice betraying her awe.

"No, just… a what?"

"Transmuter. It means you're a lot more powerful than you give yourself credit for. You need to learn to harness that, embrace it, and we'll be golden."

"Yeah?"

She nodded, had me perform the ward spell, and then motioned for me to get the next side while she ran and jumped, gliding over to the far side to take care of that one. Once done, we moved for the trap door, glancing back once at the carnage we had left behind—mostly in the form of the witch's bloodied body, as the death knights were gone.

"They won't be able to get back in without an invitation," she said as we climbed down. I glanced up to respond, quickly realizing that wasn't the gentlemanly thing to do when descending steep stairs. She had her ass out as she lowered the hatch above, and basically, I had the full view of the way the cloth was tied underneath, hugging her mound.

"Good," I said, my voice catching. "Great."

I didn't know if she caught on to my nervousness, because I looked away and quickly descended the stairs. When we reached the bottom, my aunt's secret room was in a shambles—holes blown into the walls and shelves knocked over, my aunt lying dead on the floor. "And the bodies?"

"For now, leave it." She strode past me, easily tossing aside a fallen shelf that should've taken the two of us to move. "Right now, I'm starving."

"Oh, actually, there's food already made." I pushed

ahead, opening the door for her and grinning like a horny teenage boy. She saw it right away and chuckled but nodded her appreciation for my move with the door.

"Lead the way, my lord."

I laughed, then wondered if she was teasing me or thought I could be a lord. Considering my clothes and this house, it could be an easy mistake. Nothing that needed to be addressed at the moment, I figured, so led her down to the kitchen.

# 5

I couldn't believe how much food Ebrill was devouring. As if she hadn't eaten in days. Then again, she was a gargoyle. As far as I knew, she had always been a statue so had never eaten, or else she'd been a statue for a long time, but once been awake? The best way to find out, I decided, was to ask her.

"So, all of th—"

"No," she said, mouth full, crumbs flying.

"Excuse me?"

"You want answers. I want to satiate my hunger. My want wins." She glanced over, took a bite of a sausage that she held in her hand, and added, "When I'm done, I'll explain to the best of my recollection. Wine."

"I'm not taking orders, or whining, or… what?"

"Get me a glass of wine!"

While usually the bossy woman thing didn't turn me on, something about it coming from a gargoyle was an entirely different story. I smiled as if she had just complimented my package, then turned to find a bottle of wine.

I found a wine fridge or whatever they're called in the pantry, took out a bottle, and uncorked it. Moving back to her, I noted how she was sensually licking her lips, eyes moving to meet mine as she did so.

"Two glasses," she said, leaning with elbows on the kitchen island in a way that made it difficult not to stare at her very exposed cleavage. She continued to eye me as I poured, then cocked her head, motioning me over. I went, holding out a glass for her to take. She put her hands on my chest, grinned, and then moved them down toward my abs. Then, taking the glass and raising it, she said, "Thanks."

I looked down and realized she had just wiped sauce from the glazed chicken on my shirt. "Really?"

She chuckled and held out the glass. I clinked mine against hers, as annoyed as I was.

"You find me sexy, don't you?" she asked. "Even… like this?"

I sipped and allowed my eyes to roam over her, as she did the same to me. As odd as it was to be staring at an actual gargoyle, I wasn't the least bit scared anymore, or even confused. The only emotions running through me were pure lust and infatuation.

I decided to tell her so.

Only, my aunt had just died and my girlfriend had turned out to be evil. We had killed a witch—or rather, I had watched this gargoyle decapitate her right in front of me. Maybe telling her I wanted to bend her over this kitchen island and fuck her raw wasn't the best move, just yet.

"You are stunning," I said, going for a complimentary but safe route.

"I see." She took a sip of her wine while eyeing me. "What are these clothes? This house? It's so… odd."

"Not what you're used to?"

She shook her head with a long sigh. "It doesn't seem like it, but truth be told, I'm not sure. Everything's blurry. Not my vision, but the memories." With a long look my way, she motioned for me to follow.

We made our way to an adjoining visiting room where she sat back on a posh couch, spilling some wine and not seeming to care. She sat like a lady, but after a moment, looked at me and then motioned to the seat at her side.

"I don't want to have to yell to be heard," she said.

Certain that wasn't a legitimate concern, I took the seat and smiled, drinking more of my wine. "You're sure they can't get past the wards?"

"Unless they're invited in, yes. Which makes me have to ask—"

"Please, don't." I grimaced, then sighed. "The one with the white hair. She was my girlfriend, until tonight."

"Ah."

"Apparently, she'd been setting all this up, planning for it… I don't know."

Seeing how distraught I was, Ebrill put a hand on my leg and leaned in. "She might have been being used the whole time, you don't know."

I nodded, then frowned. "How much… do you know?"

"About my past?" She glanced up. "I know the other woman's name is Kordelia, and remember that she has a special sort of magic."

"You knew how to do the wards," I pointed out.

She nodded. "Yes. A certain amount of magic makes sense to me, as if it's part of life. Yet, I feel distant."

"You have no idea how long you were in stone? Or if you even had a life before?"

"I definitely had a life." She set her now-empty glass down. "I know more than just her name. Kordelia and I were something like… lovers."

I both perked up at this image and felt deflated at the idea that my chances with her were shot. Which made me laugh.

"What's funny?"

"Sorry, just… Damn." I ran a hand through my hair, then placed it on hers, which was still on my leg. It was only a friendly gesture as I explained, "For some reason, I was imagining—sorry, but I might as well confess—imagining the two of us together."

"And that's funny?"

"No, but you said—about Kordelia, I mean."

She eyed me while gripping my hand with hers from beneath, then started moving it up my leg. "That doesn't mean we're off limits."

"Oh?"

I looked down, watching our hands move to my inner thigh, and felt the blood rushing to my crotch. "But you… Oh." Her hand had brushed against the lower side of my package, but she pulled it back then, turning to take my hand in both of hers.

"The past is a blur, for now," she said. "I remember her laughing. I remember her holding me, and me her. The way her lips felt on mine, and… I feel an emptiness no statue can fill."

"An emptiness no woman can fill?"

She frowned, laughed, and then gently slapped me. "Not what I meant."

I grinned. "Joking."

This time, she put my hand on her leg, and leaned back, though not all the way as her wings didn't fully allow that. Her eyes sparkled as if daring me, trying to see how brave I was. If she thought I was going to back down, she had another think coming. Sure, my mind was going in circles, but she had saved my life. She had kicked my old, crazy girlfriend to the curb, and as far as I could remember I had never seen a woman so beautiful, horns and wings included.

My hand moved along her thigh, feeling the tough but soft skin. I set my glass aside, then leaned in and allowed my other hand to join, the first going instead to her side and wrapping around her back as I scooted closer. My right hand met cloth, and I hesitated.

"Is this too soon?" I asked.

She nodded. "Testing you."

"What?" I pulled back, confused.

"I had the sense that part of my power lay in the realm of seduction—of bending the will of others to get what I want—but wasn't sure. You proved in part that it's true, but also that you are strong-willed."

"Isn't it possible that I simply thought you were attractive and…" Even as the words came out, I knew that was only half of it. Considering what we'd been through, me making a move like this really didn't make a lot of sense unless I factored in some sort of attraction spell like she was talking about. "Damn, so you're like… some sort of succubus."

"No." She sat up, taking my hands and holding them

while staring into my eyes. "I'm no demon, I promise you that."

"A gargoyle can't be both?"

"I don't know, but I can tell you what I am or am not, and I'm definitely no demon, especially not one that would suck your life or whatever via sex."

"Only one way to find out." I winked, squeezing her hands.

She frowned. "I might have to see if there's a way to dim the effects of my powers."

I laughed, hearing myself. "Yes, that might be smart."

"That, or get it out of the way to cut the tension." She stood and started for the door. "But first, we need to figure out a game plan, and probably see about teaching you some more spells. We need to be ready in case they find a way around those wards."

"But you said they couldn't."

"What do I know?" She laughed and held the door for me this time. "I can't even remember how I got here. Better to be prepared, though, in case."

# 6

"Your ex was looking for something, right?" Ebrill started as we worked our way back to the room where my aunt had died. "Did she give any indication of what that might be?"

"She mentioned something, more than once. The word, what was it. Hona? Something like that."

Ebrill glanced over and frowned. "Liahona?"

"That's it!" I couldn't help but notice the worry in her eyes. "You remember?"

"Something about protecting that thing," Ebrill said. "Nothing more."

We entered the room and froze.

"She was here when we left… right?" I stared at the spot where my aunt's body had been. It was now an empty spot on the floor, the shape of her body outlined by the debris surrounding it. "I'm not going crazy. I'm not."

"As far as I know, both are true."

"Bodies don't get up and walk away. Not in reality…" My eyes met hers, a nervous chuckle following. "Then again, in my reality magic doesn't exist and statues certainly don't come to life."

"I was more than a statue, before I was a statue."

I frowned. "And that helps?"

"Maybe it does, maybe it doesn't. But, what do we know?"

Racking my brain, I shrugged, feeling hopeless. "This was my aunt's house. She apparently knew some magic and passed some of it to me. Or, the ability to learn more, maybe?"

"And if this was her house, we have to assume that she knew something about me," Ebrill added.

"Why?"

"Because Kordelia and I were statues on her roof." She began looking among the fallen objects. "That has to mean something. Maybe we can find a clue as to why."

"Now that you mention it, your style doesn't exactly fit her taste. Knowing that she was into magic, and that you came to life, she must have brought you in from somewhere else."

"The odd part of that being that she never brought me to life," Ebrill replied.

"Maybe she did, but your memory resets each time?"

Ebrill considered this, pausing in her search, but then shook her head. "I wouldn't know if that were the case, but I don't think so. Bits of memories are returning, and none relate to anything in this time period. Nothing with the woman whose corpse we saw here on the way down."

"Bringing us back to the question of where the hell her body went." Something she had said caught my interest, though. "Wait, time period?"

"Yes. I see men and women in a very different style of dress, riding horses and carrying swords."

"Actually, that's fascinating. You're describing what could be a medieval time, maybe, which kind of checks out with your armor... what little you have."

She turned my way, eyebrow arched. "You don't think it's enough?"

I gulped, eyes moving along her hips. "From the perspective of a young man such as myself, it's the perfect amount."

That earned me a laugh. She returned to her search but paused only a moment later, shaking her head.

"This isn't the place," she said, heading for the door.

"It has to be. She used a spell to get back here, she—"

"No, this is the room that led to the roof, and maybe was supposed to be a safety room of sorts, but it wasn't where she would have kept her darkest, most secret treasures."

"And you have an idea where she might?"

"I... know where I would, if I were her."

Or so she thought. We moved along the various passages for what felt like hours, her running a hand along walls. She stopped to listen to the house at times, and then muttered curses. I didn't mind initially, considering what a view I had. While I felt bad for staring so much at first, this lady was so beautiful it almost felt like a crime not to. She was focused on finding answers, but my mind was more interested in the distraction from all of this that burying my face between her breasts would be.

As we were passing my room, I remembered the stains her fingers had left on my shirt and said, "Just a sec."

"A what?"

"One moment." I stepped in, went to my suitcase and found a new shirt. I quickly took off the old one, then noticed her looking at me to the extent that now I felt like the eye candy.

"Not bad, my lord."

"Why do you call me that?"

She grinned as I put my shirt on, and said, "For the fun of it. You're clearly not a lord, no offense, but I find men enjoy being put up on a pedestal. Do you not?"

"If you mean you're flirting with me, I'll take it."

Her laugh was pleasant and every bit as seductive as her look. "I have a feeling we'll be spending a lot of time together, Jericho. Trust me, we'll have our chance."

At that, she turned to investigate my room, then paused briefly at the window where Steph had entered. My mind was racing as it tried to process what she had just said, the pressure in my pants showing that at least part of me had taken it to heart. In her mind, it was a foregone conclusion that we would end up fooling around? I didn't know what to think about that, except for a big, fat 'wow.' Steph had been cute in that sit and spin, young college chick way, but this was a fully developed woman, and so much more.

A fucking gargoyle woman.

Feeling a sudden chill, I found my red jacket and threw it on, too, then went to her beside the window.

"I've been thinking," she said, and took my hand. Warm tingles ran up my arm and the pressure in my pants increased. She didn't seem to notice, thankfully, but I pushed my hips back in hopes of making it less obvious.

"Yeah?"

"Your aunt knew about your powers? As a transmuter, I mean."

I frowned, trying to figure whether my aunt might have known. "It's possible, sure. Maybe she spoke with my mom about it, or her magic had a way of telling her."

"Therefore, maybe she would have passed on something more to you than just powers, but… known you could find a way to get what she wanted you to find? Maybe the item, or, who knows… but something."

"You're saying I should try to change my surroundings to somehow find whatever it is we're looking for, based on my aunt possibly knowing this would be the case?"

Ebrill nodded, glancing over with hopeful eyes. "It's worth trying."

I nodded and then glanced around, wondering how best to do this. My first try was with holding my hand up, making the screen appear, and hoping for some transmuter language to appear. No such luck. Maybe it only worked for new spells I needed to learn.

Since that didn't work, I only had one other idea, although I didn't like it.

"Can you wait outside?" I asked. "In the hall, I mean."

"Why?"

"It's just… embarrassing."

"You need to get naked or something to transmute?" She grinned. "Go ahead."

"God. Nothing like that, but… Whatever, don't laugh." I went for the bed, sat near the headboard, and pulled my legs up to my chest. Ignoring her look of confusion, I closed my eyes and started rocking as I had all those times as a child. Focusing my thoughts on my surroundings and my aunt, I tried telling the house to reveal its secrets to me, to give me a hint, at least.

"Are you sure getting naked wouldn't be the better option?" Ebrill asked.

I laughed, shushed her, and focused.

In my mind, the house answered. Opening my eyes to see Ebrill staring in awe, I saw the response had actually come. Floating there before me was a light like the one my aunt had created as she was dying. Only, this time it started to float around and then lead me. When I sat there staring in confusion, it even moved back my way, took on a sort of animal shape—small, kind of round with a pointed back—and then moved again.

Ebrill turned to me, pointed, and asked, "Did you just create a… hedgehog familiar?"

"Kind of? For some reason, as I was making it happen, images of Sonic the Hedgehog kept popping into my head. Maybe because I wanted it to go faster?"

"I don't understand anything you just said, but we should follow your hedgehog."

She had a point. I jumped out of bed, going with her in pursuit of the light. Apparently, the familiar, or whatever it was, hadn't been the only thing my little transmuter exercise had changed about this place. It soon became clear that either I had totally misremembered the hallways of this house, or the light had led us down a turn that hadn't been there before. The next turn, too, and when we entered a hallway lit by an eerie green glow that led to stairs descending to a basement, I was sure of it.

Not any old basement, or one that even began to fit with the glamour of the house. This was more like a cave, with its rock walls and jagged stone floor. In the center the stone rose into a pedestal, where a book rested at the top.

"The Llyfr Sillafu," Ebrill said, looking at the cover. At my look of confusion regarding the strange symbols on the book's cover, she explained, "Done in the Nennian alphabet."

"Looks like runes in video games," I replied. "If I still had my damn phone, I'd be able to look it up."

She scrunched her nose in confusion but ignored the comment and stepped up to the book. "We should try simple ones at first, I suppose. Here, this one—"

"Wait," I interrupted. "Explain why you know the Nennian Alphabet... and what that is."

"I... don't know." She thought for a moment, then her eyes lit up. "Ah, but the second—it's Welsh."

"Welsh? You know Welsh?"

She shrugged. "Apparently. I'm fairly certain we're speaking it at the moment."

I laughed. "Forgot about that. My transmutation magic sort of helps me translate, so that we can understand each other. I used to think I was crazy so I never really told anyone, but... yeah, it's always done that."

"It's more than that, I think," she replied. "You know magic, and there's something about Avalon and the connection between all magic users—you understand what we say because of your connection to magic, as would anyone else in the connection."

"No shit?"

She gave me a pleased nod. "So, let's try you with this spell. Move your hand like this," she lifted a hand, fingers spread, "and say 'tarian.' Got it?"

I tried, and this time the word rolled off my tongue on

the first go. A line of gold trickled from my fingers in response.

"What was it?" I asked.

"Shield," she replied. "Although I'm not sure if this one will act like an actual shield."

"Or maybe a defense boost," I said, holding my hand up to see my screen. Sure enough, defense showed a plus three in parenthesis. "That's the one."

"In that case, there might be another spell that gives you an actual shield." She started flipping through the pages, but my focus was still on my screen.

"Whoa," I said, watching as the 'Level One' words lit up and then changed. "I just leveled up."

"You what?"

"I have levels, and I guess because of using that spell, I leveled up." I went to the book, stared at the page in front of me, and tried something. Sure enough, the page appeared in my screen. Only now, the writing made sense to me and the symbol for my hand—when necessary—was with it, and the level of the spell. "Yes! I can keep track of these, and this one is level two, so…"

"Tell me what it says. I'll see if I can guess what it does."

"Elfenol Streic," I said, making a fist as the symbol showed and hoping it had something to do with an elf. Instead, options popped up around my fist showing the four elements.

"Careful," Ebrill said. "That's an elemental strike. You should be able to use that with weapons, too, where you can imbue them with the ability to have fire, ice, etc., although the effect likely fades the moment you cast something else."

I looked at my fist, then shook it out, dismissing the idea. The last thing I needed at the moment was to accidentally burn my aunt's house down.

"If you've leveled up…" She eyed me, then glanced to the stairs.

"Right, let's try the other gargoyle again." I started for the stairs, but she caught me.

"Her name is—"

"Kordelia, I know. Sorry. Let's try to wake Kordelia."

She smiled, nodded, and we made our way back to the roof.

# 7

We were emerging onto the roof when a rumbling sounded, followed by a distant explosion. I poked my head up to see fire, or what I thought was fire. Flames licked the sky but not the trees or other buildings nearby. In fact, the fire was clearly meeting an invisible barrier, spreading out, then fading away.

"An attack?" I asked.

Ebrill emerged from behind and stood with me looking out over the attacks as more came. She nodded. "They'll try. The wards will either hold, or they won't."

"As a level two mage, I wouldn't think my wards would hold up long against whatever's out there."

"That shows how little experience you have with any of this. Your wards aren't based on your power alone, but likely tied to some power of this house. Not the walls and all that, but some setup I imagine your aunt put in place to enhance defensive spells."

"And we still haven't gotten into how you know all of this, exactly."

She grimaced. "If only I knew. But… more is coming back. A coven, a group of ladies who worked together to protect an ancient magic."

"That's… big."

She nodded. "It seems it would have been. Bigger if I could remember more of the details, but for now, let's give this a go. Better to have all the help we can get, in case that attack breaks through."

We walked over to the other statue, watching as more attacks came and more explosions of fire and other elements were repelled by the invisible force created by our wards. At one point I swear I saw winged creatures flying about in the night, but when I looked again, they were gone.

"I'd think they would be worried about the police or… fire department," I said, coming to a stop next to the statue of Kordelia. "But I imagine you're going to tell me that somehow this isn't visible to them—to civilians, I guess."

Her look of confusion was enough to remind me that, wherever she came from, police and fire departments hadn't likely been a thing.

"What I mean is, will others see the magic?"

"Ah." She pursed her mouth in thought, then shook her head. "I'd think not, if your aunt set it up that way. You might be able to sense concealment wards, actually. They basically act to hide anything she might be doing in that regard, for research or practice, but also would work to conceal attacks such as this from prying eyes."

"Gotcha."

I turned to the statue and tried as I had before. This time, the option for "Awaken" showed on the screen, but when I tried to select it, no go. Thinking that maybe it was a matter of focus, I closed my eyes, focused, then tried again.

Nothing.

"What's the problem?" she asked.

"Still not letting me, is all."

Her frown deepened as she mumbled something under her breath. "Well, try again."

"Ebrill…"

"Do it!"

I made another attempt, but without any luck. I sighed, watching as a flicker of green hit the barrier and snaked across it in all directions before fading. I shook my head.

"Then we'll come back again after more practice. Or…" She took a step back, held out her hands. "Practice here. Level up here. Come on, come at me."

"I…"

"This is as good a spot as any to attempt your elemental strike." She spread her wings, braced herself, and said, "Give it your best shot."

"I don't want to hurt you."

"Try." Her mischievous, cocky grin almost made me hope to land a strike. Nothing crazy, but enough of a shock to keep her from being too smug.

"Elfenol Streic," I said, holding up my fist and sliding it toward the lightning option before charging in.

She was right, of course. I didn't stand much of a chance. For one, I was attempting to punch a girl. That didn't sit right with me. Of course, after the first leg sweep and me hitting my head on the edge of a garden gate, then her landing a kick to my abs that sent me on my ass, I was starting to rethink my qualms about that one. The bigger issue was that I simply wasn't much of a fighter. Never had been. Raised an only child, it wasn't like I had brothers or sisters to roughhouse with. I had never taken karate classes, and the most boxing I had done was on the virtual reality boxing games, although I was pretty good at those. Going up against a real person was quite different, especially when that 'real person' was actually a badass gargoyle who clearly knew her way around a fight.

Except, when she struck me with an elbow across the sternum, I saw my opening and took it—a good punch right across the jaw.

Fuck, that hurt! My wrist stung, knuckles not much better, and no spark or lightning or anything of the sort had shot out. As I shook my hand out and cursed, I pulled up the screen to see that it had gone past its time and now had a cooldown of thirty seconds before I could use it again.

"All right, there?" Ebrill asked.

"Is this a session on beating me up, or training me?" I spat back. "Because it sure as fuck feels like the former."

She looked about to argue, but then nodded. "You're right. I'm sorry, but I thought it was important to test you, to see how far you have left to go. You have… some room to grow."

"Thanks," I said, my wrist feeling a bit better already. Still, I wasn't ready to jump back into the fight. "Why the hell did that hurt so much?"

"Ah, yes." She indicated her body in an 'I'm on display'

way, then said, "Although I'm not still made of stone, from what I can tell gargoyles move fast and are quite strong. I also get the sense that my skin is quite tough, based on Steph's fire shot before not doing much damage."

"That makes sense, actually."

"And, we need to get your powers stronger. So, come on. Try it again."

I nodded, holding up a finger so she'd give me a minute, then checked my screen. Cooldown was just finishing up, so I activated it again, this time going for ice.

"Hit me," she said, arms held out.

"No, thanks."

"Not hard, but enough to test the spell. Come on, this is necessary."

I walked up, pulled my fist back, and stared in horror as she moved to hit me instead! The *thwack* took me in the chest, and immediately I shot back, slamming her in the left breast in a way that both made her cringe and left a layer of ice over her breast.

"Ah, dammit!" she pulled back, hands on her chest, breathing heavily, eyes furious when she looked back at me again. "Get rid of it!"

Not sure what to do, I switched to fire and hit her tit again. The effect was a burst of flame that removed the ice, caused her to fall back in surprise, and left her glaring up at me.

"You told me to," I reminded her.

For a moment longer she glared, attacks against the barrier still going on around us, and then she laughed. "I thought my nipple was going to freeze off, you prick."

"You sure it didn't?" I replied with a chuckle.

Her expression turned to worry and she pulled at her

top, enough that I even caught a glimpse of her areola before averting my gaze.

"Still there," she said, covering herself again. "Lucky for you."

"And hey, the magic worked, so… there's that. You have your nipples, I have my magic spell. We all win."

That earned another laugh, and then she pushed herself up. "We *win* when you've managed to wake Kordelia."

"Right." I glanced around, feeling my confidence up a notch from where it had been, and said, "Go again?"

She grinned. "Sure, but… new rule. You don't hit me in the chest or nether regions, I leave your twig and stones alone, too. Deal?"

"Do I win in that scenario?"

"Meaning, nothing negative to the general down below. Positive, we can discuss later."

I nodded. "Deal."

We sparred again, this time with her actually helping me to understand certain fighting moves and why they would come in handy. I also worked more on the elemental strike, but with it aimed past her each time, so that we wouldn't risk freezing off her breasts, or worse.

After about an hour of this, though, I was dragging, even starting to yawn during breaks.

"You haven't slept?" she asked.

I blinked my eyes, letting them half-fall, and shook my head.

"I see." Her eyes moved to the barrier, where the attacks had stopped, I realized. "They'll return, that's for sure. But for tonight, we might be safe. Come, let's make our way back and get you to sleep."

"And you?" I asked, realizing how stupid the question was as soon as I asked it. "Ah, right. Gargoyle—stone by day, alive at night."

She nodded. "I'll keep watch the rest of the night, if you do during the day."

"Agreed, but only after..." I charged one more time, hoping to catch her off guard. She laughed, flipped me over, and knelt over me. "This..." I grunted.

Her hand gripped mine to pull me up, but I held up my other hand for a moment. Lying there, I had a realization. If I had leveled up, shouldn't increasing my stats be a function, too? I pulled up my screen, tried swiping left, and grinned to see that, sure enough, it would let me.

I groggily nodded, yawning again as we made our way inside. Guilt rose at my inability to wake Kordelia, but I knew that wasn't my fault. Soon, we would figure it out. I hoped.

When we reached my bed, I barely had the cognitive ability to manage to brush my teeth and throw off my shoes. I turned to the bed to find Ebrill sitting on its edge, looking at me, and I nodded in thanks as I collapsed beside her.

"You did well," she said, although my eyes were already closing.

The last thing I processed was her lying down next to me, draping an arm over my chest, and mumbling something about how it had been so long and how she craved the comfort of a man.

Before I could respond, even smile at the thought, sleep took me.

# 8

I've always been impressed by how real some dreams can feel, and that night's dream felt as real as could be. At first there was darkness, with me aware that I was asleep but not dreaming, exactly. Then light surged around me and my eyes adjusted until I was able to see that I stood next to a pile of hay, a barn not far off, and the sun was setting. Muddy slop under my feet pulled at my shoes as I attempted to take my first step, working my way toward a small, makeshift fence.

Something grunted behind me and I turned to see a large pig staring me down. At first, I thought nothing of this. It was a dream. A pig in a dream wasn't normal for me, but not a big deal, either.

Another step, and then more grunting came, sloshing, and I realized the pig was charging for me. My legs couldn't move fast enough, and in a matter of seconds—as my first foot lifted to go for the fence—the pig slammed into my stable leg, knocking it out from under me. I landed in the mud with a sucking sound, tasting it in my mouth like shit and grass and rotten oranges. Then the pig was there again, coming right at me.

Scrambling to get out of the way, one thought hit me as hard as a kick from Ebrill in the nuts—this wasn't a fucking dream.

No dream I'd ever had felt so real. Tasting the shit in the mud? Feeling the ache in the back of my leg where that Mr. Bacon had rammed into me? This wasn't right. I managed to reach the fence, kick back, and catch the pig on the snout with enough momentum to push myself over.

This time I landed with a thud on mud-splattered dirt and grass, where I lay staring up at the orange-speckled sky for a few moments. *Wake the fuck up,* I told myself over and over, that voice in the back of my head arguing each time that it wasn't a dream. But it had to be one, because how the hell else could this make sense?

A voice sounded. A figure blocked out the sky and then there was another. Both were speaking in a harsh tongue I didn't understand. One knelt down, sniffed me, touched my shirt, and shouted something.

Starting to freak out, I closed my eyes, again willing myself to wake up, or at least understand what the hell was going on.

Suddenly, their words made sense—not like they were speaking English, but like I could tell what they were saying even without really understanding. My powers, like with Ebrill, I imagined… although my powers had never worked in a dream.

"… men aren't fucking witches!" the first man said, who I could now see was older, with a gray mustache and peppered, long hair.

"Do you not see his clothes? His… his everything! A fucking witch, I tell you!"

It only hit me then that, maybe, just maybe, this was the same way I had been communicating with Ebrill. Now that I thought about it and had something to reference it against, her voice had this similar sensation to it, as if my mind were converting her language, and mine to hers.

If that was true, I could respond to these guys.

"I'm not a witch," I said, interrupting the second one's argument about burning me.

Both turned to me, eyes narrowing. Now even the older one nodded as he said, "Damn, you're right. A fucking witch."

"No, I—"

A thud hit me, and I was out. I would have thought that would be it, that the pain would end the nightmare. Nope. Instead I faded in and out, groggily processing being dragged across the ground, tied up in the barn, and left there while the men went off to fetch someone.

As annoying as the rope was on my wrist, this at least gave me time to think. By this point, I had accepted that it wasn't a dream. Maybe someone was using magic to get into my head? I wouldn't put it past Steph and whoever she was working with, not after the way she had betrayed me. So, this was clearly some ruse to get me to give up information, or maybe my body was sleep-walking through it, opening the door to invite the demons in again.

Whatever it was, I needed to keep my wits about me. Play it smart.

All of that thinking went out the window, though, when I noticed a small head and beady little eyes watching me from a rafter above. It vanished in a flash of little wings, leaving me to wonder how including a fairy in this little mind-fuck helped their cause. In any other situation that might have completely thrown me, but since my body was currently being cuddled by a gargoyle and I'd been fighting witches and death knights, maybe not so much right now.

What did throw me was when a set of yellow, snake-like eyes set in a green, goblin face appeared directly in front of me, glaring. Its skin was wrinkled and leathery, teeth pointed and black, and breath like the inside of a dead rat's intestines.

"This one?" the goblin asked, close enough to lick my cheek, but thank God he didn't. "Let's see if we can't get it out of him."

He was nude aside from a belt with a loincloth, but pulled out a serrated dagger from the back of his belt, holding it at my neck, letting the cold steel test my resolve.

"So, boy, which coven do you belong to?"

I stared back, not showing any weakness, resolved to find a way out of this. Clearly, denying being a witch wasn't going to work, and as I had recently found out, I actually was one. No point in lying. But I didn't belong to a coven.

His blade bit me, surely drawing blood.

"District of Colombia," I blurted out. "And it's a big fucking coven, too."

The goblin snarled and leaned in, licking his lips. "Fucking?"

Realizing my mistake in language choice, I rolled with it. "All the time. Witches, so many witches who want to fuck. Cast spells, take a break to fuck. Have dinner, then a nice fuck. It's tough being a witch, sometimes."

He chuckled but then glared again, as if remembering himself. "Why is it that I haven't heard of this District of Columbia coven?"

"Ask him," a dark, hissing voice demanded.

The goblin froze, clearly terrified of whatever it was that had spoken, then brought the knife up to my eye, pointy end right at the edge so that it was too blurry to focus on. "You belong to such a big fucking coven, you'll know, won't you? You'll know where the Liahona is."

"I don't—" The knife pinched my eyelid and I cursed.

"The Liahona," the creature snarled. "Tell me, or you lose this eye first. Then your other, followed by your tongue—"

"If you cut out my tongue, how would I tell you where it is?"

"You'd walk me to it, you nasty shit!"

Mocking the little guy probably wasn't the best move, as his eyes had just slanted into a mischievous glare, the knife twisting. Clearly, I still had no idea what a Liahona was, but since everyone kept asking about it, the thing must have been important.

"Taking you is the only way," I blurted out, not sure what to do, but knowing that would buy me time. "There's a magical barrier set up. It needs me to go through, to take it down."

"He's lying," the voice said, and the goblin shook its head, then laughed. It pulled its blade back, licked its teeth, and plunged.

In that moment, though, I used my elemental strike to freeze my bonds and break through them, then catch him with an ice punch to the elbow as I threw my head out of the way of his blade. The result was that his arm froze and snapped in two from my punch, then shattered on the ground.

The goblin shrieked, staring in confusion. I didn't stay to find out what would happen next, knowing that I didn't want to meet his colleague.

Charging out of there, I emerged to find myself surrounded by large tents, lines of them, and fires beyond. Big warriors with shades of green and even purple skin were throwing back drinks while others practiced swordplay.

I didn't waste any time wondering where I was, simply darted left and ducked under a large oak, out of the light of the nearest fire. Where I was supposed to go, I had no idea, but I knew I didn't belong here. Shouts sounded from behind and I threw myself to the ground, hoping they wouldn't see me. The cold night was so dark it was almost impossible to see anything. I pressed low, branches and rocks scraping my forearms, and crawled away from the camp as fast as possible, only stopping when I noticed eyes staring at me from the darkness ahead.

Heart racing, I froze, hoping whoever was out there hadn't spotted me. Two seconds later, a flash of steel caught my attention, then more. Forms were moving. A sudden roar filled the night and they were up and charging. My gut clenched and my hands shook as I started to push up, but they charged past me, drawing their weapons. They weren't coming for me at all, I realized, throwing myself down next to a tree, but storming the camp!

I saw one man coming from my left so went to go

right, when I slammed into the side of a charging horse, fell back, and whacked my head on a tree.

Any hint of light that had been there a moment before faded. When the noise of my harsh, wheezing breathing woke me, and then the darkness faded, I realized that someone was talking.

"Thank you, Irla," a voice said in a whisper. "You're sure he's one of ours?"

"Only what I was told," Irla replied.

"A witch?"

I processed someone approaching and blinked as my vision cleared. As far as I knew, I had a concussion and needed medical attention. Instead, I was on a thick blanket on a stone floor, this woman staring down at me. Again, I blinked, and this time I made out that she was petite and wore a gown of purple, cinched around the waist by a cord-style belt. Her fiery red hair was pulled back, and she eyed me with very blue eyes.

"You're not with us," she said, starting to turn.

"You can't just leave me here," I mumbled.

With a glance back, she scoffed, "Can't I?"

"The Liahona," I blurted out, taking a gamble. "If you leave me here, they'll get it instead of you."

That caught her attention. "You… know?"

I nodded. "And my goal is to keep them away from it. So…"

Another moment of thought, and then she was back at my side, first looking at my shirt, then kneeling to run her fingers along my jeans. "What are these clothes you're wearing?"

The answer to that question was simple, but complicated. For one, would telling her that I was from the future mess with her head, or threaten to ruin my time? The question in itself was flawed, because while this had many similarities to a medieval time of my past, there were goblin creatures and other things here, I imagined. For all I knew, I was learning that my past had these, as my present—their future—had gargoyles and demons. What I had always thought might be an aspect of my imagination was actually magic, it turned out, and my aunt was part of some magic plot where an enemy group was trying to find something before her, or she was hiding it. Frankly, nothing was simple anymore.

Instead of giving her an answer, I responded with a question. "Who are you?"

She frowned, hand still on my leg, and said, "Aerona."

I nodded, glancing at her hand on my leg, then back up at her captivating eyes, wondering what exactly was happening here and what the purpose of this whole experience was. Before I had a chance to find my answers, though, it all started to fade.

"He's leaving us," Irla said, as I felt my body fading.

A glance down confirmed this, just as a third woman entered the room. There was something special about this one, though. Somehow, I knew her.

Tall, slender, wearing a red robe drawn around her shoulders to cover the gold-plated armor beneath. Wavy black hair fell over her left shoulder. Her eyes met mine, and then I knew.

"Ebrill?" I asked, her eyes widening in surprise as I was pulled out from that world.

# 9

My eyes sprang open, staring into Ebrill's closed ones.

"Was it you? Were you there?"

Only, she wasn't moving. She was stone.

Shit, it was daytime. She had not only turned to stone but was still lying on me, arm draped over me in a way that made moving her off very awkward. In the process, I accidentally grazed her boob, only to realize how stupid a thing that was to be concerned about. She happened to be stone, it wasn't exactly the same as when she was in the flesh.

I would have to wait until nightfall to ask her about my crazy experience, apparently. How had she gotten from that strange place to where we were now? She had been human, or, actually, now that I thought about it, her ears might have been unusually pointed. Was she an elf or something similar, once upon a time? My mind was spinning with questions, my nerves rattled with the thought that I couldn't have my answers yet.

Even when night fell, for all I knew, she still wouldn't remember.

I headed for the bathroom. My limbs were stiff, my bladder full, and morning wood raged like a motherfucker. Apparently, that happens when being cuddled by a hot gargoyle and going back in time to see her and other beautiful women as… elves? The thoughts were hitting me now that I was awake, and it all sounded so much crazier.

In a world where I'd been told I was crazy for thinking I could alter my surroundings with my mind, to finding out it was magic and there was so much more… did time travel via sleep seem so out there? *Fuck it,* I decided. Might as well go with the flow and see where it took me. Speaking of flow, damn, did I have to piss. I entered the bathroom, did my best not to make a mess, and then decided to wash off the sweat that had soaked right through the back of my shirt last night.

A result of the dreams, or travel, perhaps? Meaning, my body had likely stayed here, while my mind did some crazy astral projection shit. Or… something like that. Who knew?

I undressed to take a shower, pausing at the thought that Ebrill was lying right there on the bed. Damn, the way her loincloth fell back to reveal her ass was hot, and to think she had been sleeping next to me, curled up against me! Checking out a statue… an odd moment, for sure.

At least I didn't have to worry about her sneaking a peek, although it wasn't like that really would have been a negative. Her being awake in this scenario was by far my preferred choice. As I stripped and stepped into the shower, I kept imagining her shedding the stone as she had the night before and then stepping in to join me. Shampoo cascaded down my face and I closed my eyes, instead imagining her as the elf lady version of herself. Both were sexy in their way.

I was very confused about all of this. My aunt had died on my first night in Washington, D.C. Not some fantasy land, not some place where elves or gargoyles existed, and certainly not a world where it made sense for a girlfriend to suddenly become a demon with her own little evil army.

Speaking of which, I wondered why I didn't hear any attacks. They had to know Ebrill was a gargoyle and would be asleep during the day, so this would be the best time to attack. I finished rinsing and dried off on my way to the bedroom window to pull the curtains aside and have a look.

It had to be midday, or at least late morning, judging by the angle of the sun. There were no attacks, no walls of fire or even burnt trees. Everything looked so… ordinary. Aside from the sleeping, stone gargoyle in my bed—creating a massive indentation in the mattress, I noticed—it was as if none of the night before had happened.

"Will you need breakfast?" a voice said, and my head jerked up as I realized at once that I had dropped my towel, and that Fatiha, the servant lady, stood in the doorway, staring with an amused smile.

"Yes, please." I played it cool, as if this were normal, although in my head I was shrieking, covering myself, and running into the bathroom.

She nodded, gave my package another glance, and walked off. "It will be ready in the…" She paused as she turned back. This time, her eyes went to the bed, instead. "Oh. I see you, er, made a new friend."

"The statue?"

When her eyes met mine, the smile gone. I had no doubt that she knew Ebrill was more than a statue. "Where is Gertrude this morning?"

"That..." My hands finally moved to cover myself, finding it much more awkward when she wasn't checking me out, for some reason. "Do you mind if I dress, first?"

An intense sorrow filled her eyes as she apparently took my meaning from those words. She nodded and stepped away as she added, "Tell me over breakfast."

My heart thudded as I pulled on my boxer briefs and pants, found one of my remaining three clean shirts, and headed downstairs. Was it wrong that I'd first paused to give Ebrill a kiss on the cheek? Maybe weird... I don't know, but I wanted to thank her for saving me the night before, and even though I knew she wouldn't feel it, the action felt right.

Fatiha was sitting with a rigid posture at one end of the table, toast and a jar of orange marmalade in front of her. My setting included a cup of coffee, orange juice, and a plate with sausage patties and eggs. Now that it was before me and the scent of those sausages and the coffee reached my nose, I realized how hungry I was and dove in.

When I'd eaten half of the plateful, the lady finally cleared her throat.

I looked up, finished chewing, and set my fork down. About to tell her everything, I paused for a gulp of coffee, but she held a hand up.

"I'm going to fill you in, and tell you what I assume

happened last night," she started. "Feel free to tell me when I get something wrong. In case you don't recall, I am Fatiha, and I was your aunt's closest friend. Sometimes, maybe more. But, that's not important. What you need to know, and probably already have an inkling about, is that your aunt was much more than you originally thought. She was the Searcher, the one my order had hoped would find the Liahona, an ancient item of great magical importance."

At the mention of the Liahona, I blinked, and she noticed. For a moment we stared at each other, and then I said, "That's not the first time I've heard that word."

"Gertrude mentioned it?"

"Before, and..." I shook my head. "I mean, as stupid as it sounds, a dream."

Her eyes took on an intense fascination and her hand shook as it moved for the marmalade. She took a small spoonful, and used the back of it to spread the marmalade on the bread. "And the... gargoyle?"

"Last night, we were under attack. I woke her."

Fatiha's hand froze in place, marmalade on half of the bread. "And in the dream?"

"How...?" I started but nodded.

"Gertrude is dead, then."

Again, I nodded.

She set aside the spoon, eyes staring blankly, then picked up the bread and took a bite. Just bread, no marmalade. She chewed slowly, blinked, and seemed to remember that I was there.

"Where?" she asked. "Where is Gertrude?"

"About that." I took another chug of my coffee. "I can show you where she *was*."

The expression in Fatiha's eyes went from hopeless to confusion, followed by her standing. "Show me."

With a glance of regret at my food, I took a sausage patty with me and my half-finished coffee, going with her to the room where my aunt had died and then her corpse had vanished. Along the way, I finished my patty, then my coffee as Fatiha explained that she lived in Bethesda but had known Gertrude since they were children, and had been involved in this Searcher business since my aunt had decided it was her role.

"Decided?" I asked.

"That's correct. There was a book that spoke of things beyond our belief, our comprehension, really. But she started studying them, learning... dreaming."

"I see."

"And it led to riches, but all for the cause. It led to enemies, too, and eventually she was taken in by a group known as The Order of the Mystic Moon. It's a group carried down by those first, early protectors of the Liahona. Lost to time but rediscovered in a book passed down for generations until it vanished, only to be rediscovered in the late 1800s. For years, they put pieces together, practiced spells discovered along the way, and searched for the Liahona."

"My aunt..." I let that all sink in. The idea that she was all part of this secret order and had never told us. Or maybe my mom *had* known, but thought it too weird to share? I couldn't believe my mom would have let me stay at my aunt's place if she had known, though. My parents wouldn't even let me watch *Rainbow Bright* when I was a child because they thought that show had too much to do with witchcraft. This was a whole other level.

"She discovered the gargoyles," Fatiha went on, "and brought them here, but never learned how to wake them. At times, I wondered if she was mad, if the gargoyles were nothing but statues. Then, this morning... to see one in your bed like that..."

"We didn't sleep together, I mean in that way, if—"

"Enough," she waved her hand. "It would be none of my business if you had."

I nodded, not really sure where I stood in all of this. We reached the hallway, each step feeling heavier as we approached the room. Stepping in, I frowned in confusion. The room was not at all how I had last seen it, but was completely put back in order, even with broken walls fixed.

"There." I pointed to the spot where my aunt had fallen. "But I don't... I don't understand."

"You will," a stern voice said, and there was my aunt, standing in an alcove of the room. Only, it wasn't quite her, as I could see the shelves behind her.

"A ghost?" I asked, not sure what would surprise me at this point.

"Not exactly," Fatiha said, stepping toward her, but stopping at a shelf at her side, where a jade sculpture of a small tree was kept on display. "More like her... but not her."

"I had myself linked to this Life Tree," my aunt explained, approaching us. "This isn't me, exactly, but like the essence of me. A part left behind, should you need my help."

"Considering everything that's happening," I replied, "I'd say that's a very real possibility."

"With my last breath, I transferred magic to you, and

my consciousness here. If I can guide you, I will. Fatiha..." My aunt turned to the woman, a sorrowful smile taking over. "You were my everything. I'm sorry it had to end like this."

"My best friend, my rock." Fatiha held up the tree, pricked her finger on the side of it, and chanted under her breath as she let a drop of blood fall onto the base. "I accept your sacrifice, and give of myself so that what remains may grow stronger."

With those words, my aunt faded into a ball of light that entered the jade tree.

"Okay, what the fuck...?" Cringing at the look Fatiha gave me, I added, "Sorry, but this is all too much."

I gave the tree one more glance, then turned to get out of there.

At the door, Fatiha caught up to me. "Where are you going? We have a lot to do, a lot to—"

"I just... need to think."

I was out, jogging down the street, cursing that I didn't have a phone to call a driver. Since I didn't have a car, I walked. A stranger to this city, I had no idea where I was going but that didn't stop me.

At the moment, all that mattered was being alone and away from all the crazy bullshit.

# 10

There wasn't much to think about, really. Going from thinking I was a normal guy with a girlfriend and about to go to university, only to have it all thrown upside down with magic, time travel, and now what was essentially a ghost—it was a lot to take in.

At the moment, I wanted to look at the fun architecture of the nearby houses, the trees blowing in the wind, and birds soaring by. I wanted to forget all the insanity, and focus on what had always been real, what was simple. After a bit of walking, I hopped in a taxi and paid way too much to end up at the National Mall, where I checked out some museums, stood staring at a wooly mammoth recreation for like thirty minutes, and then walked over to the Capitol Building. After that, my legs were as exhausted as my emotional state, so I found an out of the way coffee shop, grabbed a green tea, and then sat in the back with my head against the wall. After a short nap, I woke to find a tour group crowded around, kids eyeing me and chuckling. I nodded and went on my way.

From there, I thought about calling my friends or parents, but what could they do? They couldn't relate to me in this, and I had no interest in making up an answer for when they asked what I had been up to so far.

Instead, I found a food court, ate some mediocre Chinese beef and broccoli, and then started to make my way back toward the house. The summer humidity was a drag, but for a little while I welcomed it as something to focus my negative energy on rather than all the myriad other options. When I couldn't take it anymore, I found a bus that took me halfway, and then got out to walk again.

Everything around that area reminded me of pictures of Rome or Greece, although it wasn't like I had been to either to really know. The buildings had that grand, marble look, and when I stopped to look at a church, I couldn't help but feel that the West Coast got screwed with its lack of amazing architecture.

A flock of pigeons flew past. One of them landed nearby, and gave me the distinct sensation that it was watching me. More appeared as I walked on. After the third time, I noticed a figure standing at the raised side of a park, white hair blowing in the wind. At least her eyes didn't appear red anymore, or not from this distance.

Steph waited there, and I didn't turn away.

Her hands were folded in front of her, and at least she was wearing normal clothes during the day, instead of the strange renaissance getup she had worn the night before. Now she had a look that was less like a demon summoner or whatever she was, and more of a punk rock wannabe. Her gray pants with holes were paired with a low-cut red shirt with black vest over it. The whole ensemble reminded me of the old Avril Lavigne look—some singer from the nineties my dad had always pretended not to listen to.

My instincts kicked in as I approached her, eyes darting about for trouble. Every ounce of me was screaming that I needed to turn around and run, but stubbornness won out. She had been my girlfriend and betrayed me. Words needed to be had.

"The fuck, Steph?" I said, as soon as I figured I was probably within ear shot.

She laughed. "I could ask the same of you. All I wanted was to look around, to have some fun. You spoiled it."

"You killed my aunt."

"It wasn't me, exactly."

"Bullshit." I glared, then scoffed with a shake of my head. "Stop talking as if we're two normal people having a conversation. It's pissing me off."

She cocked her head, smiling. "How would you like to talk instead?"

"Like you're a traitorous bitch, a murderous piece of shit, maybe." I shrugged. "What's to stop me from ending this right here?"

"Really?" She motioned around. "Go ahead, and have fun with that, too. Have fun being the guy who beat a woman to death right here in D.C. Although, truthfully," she leaned in, smirking, "I think I could take you."

A twitch at the side of her mouth. One I recognized all too well. "You're bluffing." She frowned, confirming it, and it hit me. "That's why you're not attacking right now… because your powers aren't as strong during the day. Or maybe don't work at all."

"You don't know what you're getting into, Jericho." She stepped close, hand going out for my arm, but I pulled back instinctively. The hurt in her eyes was quickly replaced by anger. "Fuck you, okay? I'm out here risking everything to try and give you another chance. When my lips were around your cock, you think that was fake? No! I fucking lo—er, like you. Okay? And I'm telling you right now, you have this one chance to make everything right. Don't, and I can't guarantee your safety."

"Problem is, I think you're full of shit," I countered, taking another step back, eyes darting to two forms I noticed at the edge of a clump of trees in the park. "Safety? I need to find a way to be safe from you, first of all."

"You take one more step, and that will be the truest thing you've ever said."

I stared her down, held up the finger, and stepped away. "Steph, didn't you learn anything from our time dating? Take your ultimatum and shove it."

Her magic might not have been very powerful during the day, but when she pulled out a taser, I fucking knew better than to delay this any longer than was necessary. My legs were already moving, my arms pumping as I took off in a sprint, propelling myself over a parked car and right into traffic. The taser missed, but a pickup truck almost connected. I fell back, feeling the wind gush by, then took off across the street, hoping to God the cars would stop. A gunshot sounded. A bullet hit a red sedan and caused the driver to swerve, hitting another car. As bad as I felt, I didn't have time to wait around and check on everyone. Apparently, Steph's friends were smart enough to not rely on only magic.

How stupid could I be? What had caused me to think it was okay to walk around in public after the previous night? It was beyond me.

I ducked around a deli, glancing around for options, when I saw a blue Volvo come around the corner. Fatiha was driving and waving for me, mouthing what I could only assume was, "Get in!"

Another gunshot went off as she pulled up and popped open the door for me, ducking as the rear passenger window shattered with another shot.

"Quickly," she hissed.

I didn't need to be told twice, and threw myself in, legs still behind me as I worked to get the door shut. She slammed a small crystal onto the dash and sat up, pedal to the metal. Another shot hit, and she ducked, then said, "Wards, dammit! Do you know them?"

Without even thinking, I shouted, "Ddiogelu!" and did the hand motion, our car lighting up so that the next two shots that hit a split-second later simply rebounded.

"There we go," she said, grinning, and laughed as she did another U-turn, went over a curb, and peeled out as we made our way out of there.

# 11

"Your life isn't going to be what you thought," Fatiha said, turning the wheel hard and glancing over. "At this point, you have a choice to make."

"Live or die?" I asked, glancing back over my shoulder.

"On a basic level, yes. But I mean that you need to commit, or likely die. The third choice is to go over to their side, but then I'd have to kill you, of course."

I laughed, only to see she wasn't smiling. Not a joke, apparently.

"You have nothing to worry about," I said. "Maybe death, but not me switching sides. My aunt was committed. I'm even more so."

"We'll see about that."

A screeching sounded and two cars appeared, closing in on us. Steph wasn't giving up so easily. What I couldn't have expected was how well Fatiha handled the drive through the city. She seemed to know every turn, every in and out of public parking lots, and was quick at the wheel.

In the parking lot of a church, the enemy cars drew close enough that they opened fire, seemingly aimed for our tires, but Fatiha drove right through a gate, came peeling out on a road where we almost flipped while a truck swerved to avoid us, and then we were going down a hill, turning again and again, and there was no sign of them.

We also didn't seem to be headed for the house. "Where are we?"

"Taking you on a tour," she replied, and winked.

I shifted in my seat to see the Capitol Building in the distance, a sign that said 14th Street, and then Dupont Circle.

"This is… I mean…"

"Yes, I'm taking you to see the White House."

"I took a walk, saw some of the city."

"Doesn't matter," she said, waving the comment off. "We need to be somewhere public. Right about now they're going to look for you around the house, and as you might have figured by their use of guns, their magic is weak during the day."

"Mine isn't."

She nodded. "Observant. That's the problem with dark magic, even more so with shadow magic. During the day, they aren't much better than common criminals, trying to shoot up the city. If we're in a well-guarded, heavily populated area, our chances of survival rise drastically."

That made sense. "But what about the car and the ward on it? Couldn't we just hide in the car, or drive through whatever they throw at us?"

"Wards are temporary," she replied. "The ones on the house are amplified by the same power that will allow your aunt's Life Tree to work. Out here, not so much. A few good shots, and your ward breaks."

"A public place it is, then." I sat back, watching the tall buildings as we drove closer. D.C. was unlike anything I'd experienced back in Oregon. While Portland was a big city and had the most amazing bookstore, it was like apples and oranges to D.C. Soon, we were walking along the area next to the old war building. We took a tour of some apartment across the way that held significance but didn't matter to me in the slightest at the moment, and then ate at the restaurant on top of the W, where we had a great view of the Treasury building and, past it, the White House.

She ordered meatloaf for herself and insisted I try the crab cakes. We sat back, taking it all in. A moment to relax.

"I'm going to miss her," Fatiha said.

"Ah, yes. Me too." I indicated her pocket. "But you have..."

"The tree?" She allowed a smile. "It's something, sure. But imagine, if you will, having a favorite hamburger, and then one day being told you can hold a toy version of the hamburger, but never taste the real thing."

"That's got to be one of the worst—"

"I know, I know. But you get the picture. It's not the same as having the real her." Hand going to her pocket, she nodded in appreciation as the waiter brought us waters, then watched him walk off. "Ask me."

"What?"

"Why here. Ask me why I brought you here." She turned back to me, sipped her water, and waited.

"Wh—"

"Because it was the last place Gertrude and I went out to. We mostly didn't go out anymore, at least not when it could be helped. But she had made a discovery, about the time when she told me you would be coming. So, we had to celebrate."

"Was the discovery… me?"

"You?" Her smile faded. "I… actually hadn't considered that. She kept a lot of her work private, only filling me in on what was necessary. And she did talk about your coming quite often, but I never put the two together."

"You two—"

"Holy shit."

I turned to her and frowned. "What?"

"I can't believe I didn't put the two together before. Here I was thinking we had a lead on another gargoyle or something, or finally anything to do with the actual location of the Liahona. But it was you." She turned to me, looking me up and down, and then laughed. "You're the piece of the puzzle. But sorry, you were going to say?"

"Just…" I ran a hand over my chin, massaging it, not sure how to take her burst of surprise and the way she was suddenly looking at me. "I was going to say that you two sounded very busy. Doing what, exactly?"

"Traveling. We found those gargoyles, Ebrill being one, apparently—"

"And the other is Kordelia."

"You don't… say." She eyed me, took another sip, then nodded as the food arrived. When the waiter was gone again, she leaned in, lowering her voice. "Those names aren't completely alien to me, you should know."

"You've seen them before."

She nodded. "In a book, one that Gertrude found. We can ask her about it sometime," she tapped her pocket, "find out where the book is for the other names. But yes, Ebrill and Kordelia were two witches who are said to have been part of the magical war that actually ended much of magic on Earth."

"How so?" I asked.

"That's something we'll have to ask Ebrill."

"If she ever gets her memory back." I took a bite of my crab cake and leaned back, enjoying it. Perfection.

"What—er, what's going on with you two?" Fatiha glanced over, as if she knew this was a weird question to ask.

"Does it matter one way or another?"

She shook her head. "Curious, is all."

"I think… we're bonding?" Leaning forward and lowering my voice now, I added, "After seeing her in the dream… more so."

"Good." She nodded, took another bite of her meatloaf, chewed, and swallowed while we sat in silence, me wondering if this was really good in her mind. I finished my first and second crab cakes, letting my mind wander to my buddies back home and stories they used to tell. This guy Rob had always bragged about fingering girls, as if that was better than fucking, and how many fingers he could get in. Then there was Jason, who had brought us to his house one day and put a video on the projector of him and some girl fucking. I wanted to look away, but at least his dick was in her most of the time. All until the end, when there was a closing image of her with the tip in her mouth making a peace sign. Crazy bastards. I couldn't help but imagine how they would react if I told them a fucking gargoyle had come alive and cuddled me.

Not that I would, but imagining their reactions was fun. At the thought of Ebrill so close, I had to change how I was sitting so the bulge forming wouldn't be so obvious. Fatiha noticed and gave me a humored glance.

"Shouldn't we be, I don't know, trying to find other ways to wake Kordelia?" I asked, trying to get the focus off me.

"Want to get me back there, is that it? Just the..." She froze, licked her lips, then muttered, "Shit."

"What?"

"It's... I took one of my medications earlier. Has this added effect of making me say things."

"Like just now."

She cocked her head and nodded. Then eyed me closely, waiting for me to say something. Suddenly, she was up and motioning to the waiter. "Check, please."

We left without another word about it. I wondered if the moment had been her hitting on me or something else. At her age, it felt off, but... kind of hot? The longer the silence continued, though, the more certain I was that it was exactly what happened. She wanted me, or at least her medication made her think she did.

I glanced over. Her eyes met mine, and we shared an awkward smile.

"So... what now?" I asked.

"When night falls, we try to wake the second, like you said."

The elevator door *dinged* open and we exited, turning right to make our way over along Fifteenth Street. Of course, I had meant what would happen between the two of us, but I left it alone. If she wanted to pretend it hadn't happened, I could do that.

"I'm getting an ice cream," Fatiha said, indicating the ice cream cart on the corner. Considering the heat, it sounded perfect. "Then maybe a drink, in Gertrude's memory. You?"

"I'll go for the ice cream," I said. Grieving didn't come easy for me, considering I had barely known the woman. While Fatiha was doing a good job masking her emotions, her eyes showed that she was clearly distraught, so I added, "My treat."

"Don't you start." She waved me away and pulled out a purse stuffed with cash and cards. "If there's one area we won't have to worry about, it's money."

I nodded, not sure if I had ever seen so much money in one place. Upon seeing the surprise on my face, she shrugged. "Your aunt has always been very generous. Now that she's gone, maybe more so. Her remnant—let's call it that—gave me instructions after you left. She wanted her fortune to go on for the two of us. To pursue what she started, but never managed to finish."

"Meaning, I'm rich but can't use it."

She chuckled, nodding. "You can, but draw too much attention to yourself and you'll likely be dead by the next morning. We need to focus on the objective—find the Liahona before the enemy, and ensure it can never be used by them."

"Ensure how?"

She weighed me up with a penetrating look before turning back to the road, and replying, "Do what those of old never could do. Destroy it."

"If it's so powerful, couldn't we use it to defeat the enemy?"

She shook her head. "It has a way of affecting its user. Making the best of us mad for power."

"So, we get it, destroy them, then destroy it. Yeah? But how does it work, and how do we destroy it? Throw it into Mt. Doom, I'm guessing."

The reference was lost on her, as she shook her head. "I don't know of any such mountain, but no, and I don't have the answer to that question."

With a solemn nod, I cleared my throat and looked out at the many sweaty tourists, a statue of a man on a horse, and several protesters in front of the White House. All of those people thought what they were doing was important, and that this building they were looking at housed one of the most powerful men in the world. How little they knew. According to what I was hearing, the mission I was taking on was of more importance than anything any president had ever done and had the potential to give me more power than anyone.

An overwhelming thought, for sure.

"That should do," Fatiha said, eyes lingering on my face longer than seemed natural. After a moment, she said, "You know, you have some of her in you."

"My aunt?"

She nodded. "Maybe it's the magic, the sense of adventure in what's about to come. I don't know. But, I see it."

I smiled and turned back to watch the activists on the White House lawn.

"Come on," she said, indicating the sun's low position in the sky. "Best get back before dark."

“They won’t be waiting anymore?”

“Oh, they might be. I’m hoping they’ve thinned out, but also, I’ve had time to come up with a plan.” She grinned, pushed herself up, and then offered me a hand. I nodded, pushed myself up on my own, and followed her back to the car.

# 12

Fatiha passed a corner where the house was visible, paused at the stop sign, and kept going two more blocks. Deep shadows already spread out across lawns, sunset nearly upon us.

"What I don't get," I said as we exited the car, "is why they didn't come after me right away when I left the house."

"They actually believed they had a shot at converting you, is my only guess." She checked around and indicated a way through a stranger's yard. We moved at a brisk pace.

"So, you think they have the place on constant watch?"

"I can't see why they wouldn't, at this point."

"Tarian," I said, making the gesture and feeling glad about my defense going up. As I was about to cast another, Fatiha put a hand on my forearm and shook her head. "No need."

"But if we're going up against them…"

"Gertrude was smart—at times I thought paranoid—

but, it turns out… smart." Indicating for me to follow, she led me along a stone wall that led to a vine-covered wall. We hopped over the stones to the grass on the other side and then started running in a crouch. We ducked behind two trees in a clump of willows. "Smart, because she made secret passages."

At that, Fatiha strode over to the vines, moved something from the base, and then reached past the greenery. A moment later, a section of the wall *creaked* and she ducked through the vines, vanishing from sight. I looked around and then followed, not sure what to expect.

The vines gave resistance at first, but then I was through, ducking into a narrow walkway between two walls. We soon reached a dead end, but Fatiha kept going, moving the wall to our right to reveal a hole where a ladder led the way down.

"A bit crude, but it serves its purpose." She went first, me following close behind, and soon we were running along through the basement, coming up into a closet. Fatiha gave me a look as if she were going to pin me against the wall in there and show me her version of seven minutes in heaven, but instead checked the door and led us out. The fantasy about getting with such an older woman felt strange to me, but as I imagined her teaching me with her experience, I couldn't ignore the temptation… and curiosity.

My first move was to go to one of the front windows, to see what we were dealing with. I stayed close to the curtain, barely peeking out, and saw several pairs of red eyes appear in the shadows of the trees in the neighbors' yards. The pink of the sky had faded to a dull, dark blue, meaning we had made it in at the perfect time.

"No more wandering off, agreed?" Fatiha demanded. When I nodded, she said, "Good. Go check on your friend so you're there when she wakes. Get her up to speed while I check on your aunt."

"On her remnant, you mean."

"Ah, right. Yes."

I watched her walk off, wondering if I should be worried, but then jogged up to my room. Night was nearly upon us, after all. A cracking sounded at the exact moment I entered. Ebrill stretched as the glow faded from her eyes, and she turned in bed to look at me.

"What're you doing way over there?" she asked.

"I..." I started but didn't know what to say when she motioned me over. For a moment, I stood there, enthralled by the seductive look in her eyes, then I walked over, brushed aside some stone, and sat next to her.

She sat up and wrapped her arms around me. "I missed you."

"Ebrill, we... I mean..."

The look of realization in her eyes told me exactly what was happening. She must have had a dream about me, one where we were more than real life. Maybe even one where we had been intimate?

Cocking my head with that thought in mind, I looked at her. She blushed and looked away.

"Tell me about your dream," I said, teasing.

Her eyes met mine and she said, "Tell me about yours, first."

I sat up, pulling away slightly. "Wait, you... it was you, wasn't it?"

She gulped, then nodded. "I don't remember much, but now… now I remember that day when you showed up. You were a mystery, causing such a stir, only to fade away. Much is still a blur, but, the way you looked at me. Of course, I've had dreams of you since then, you and your sultry eyes." She turned, took my face in her hands, and stared into my eyes. Hers, I now noticed, were more of a purple than the dark brown I had originally thought them to be. Purple to match her lips, which were moving toward me. She gently placed a kiss on my cheek, then smiled as she pulled back.

"That place," I said, dazed, "do you know what it was?"

She sighed, shaking her head. "I'm getting bits and pieces. Just images, but I'm certain we were searching."

"For the Liahona."

She perked up. "Yes, exactly. You…you've been busy?"

"There's someone I think you should meet." Taking her by the hand and guiding her up, as apparently, we were close enough for that now, I led her out of there, but paused. "Sorry, do you… I've been running around all day. One minute, okay?"

I ran into the bathroom, took a quick piss—which was hard to do, considering the semi-chub she had left me with after that kiss—washed my hands, and headed back to her.

"Good?" she asked, and I realized I had totally not even thought about closing the door.

"Er, before when you were stone, I hadn't bothered. And I guess I didn't think…"

"You were walking around naked while I was stone? A bit creepy."

I laughed. "Sorry?"

"Well, creepy and sort of sexy." She shrugged, took my hand again, and gestured for me to lead the way.

"Okay, so while you were sleeping, a few things happened," I told her, and went into my day, finishing up with us arriving in the dining room, where Fatiha waited.

"This is the one?" Ebrill asked, but Fatiha stood frozen, serving tray in hand, jaw dropping as she stared.

"Yes, and she's not usually so… awestruck?"

"Sorry," Fatiha said, snapping out of it. "Please, help yourself to the food. You must be famished. Wow, a real, live gargoyle here at my table."

"At your pleasure," Ebrill said with a slight curtsy, then started picking at some grapes, before eyeing the cheese and sliced corned beef.

"My apologies, I just threw together whatever I could find."

"It's perfect." Ebrill found a seat, wings folding halfway behind her, and continued to eat, eyes going back and forth between us as we stared. "So…We need a plan."

"Maybe we should speak with Gertrude, see what she can tell us?" Fatiha offered.

"Wait, your aunt?" Ebrill asked me.

"Did I forget that part?" I grimaced. "Well, she did pass on, sort of, but left something of herself behind. A remnant, you could say."

"That's… powerful magic."

"It is," Fatiha confirmed. "Which is why I think it's important that Jericho keeps learning from her, as much as possible."

"And the Liahona?" Ebrill asked. "Have we located it?"

Fatiha shook her head. "But if you've awoken, I would say we're one step closer as a team. We know they will attack again tonight, likely with stronger forces. We must prepare, but first, Jericho, your aunt is waiting to speak with you."

The idea of conversing with a remnant of my aunt gave me the willies, but I nodded and glanced toward the hallway that led to where I had last seen her.

"That won't be necessary," Fatiha said, pulling the jade tree from her pocket and running her finger along it.

Green light shone along the branches, swirling around and creating a space before forming into the figure of my aunt. She took on her natural colors, clothes and all, and eyed first me, then Ebrill.

"Well, I'll be…" Excitement shone in her eyes and she moved forward as if to touch Ebrill to see if she was real, but her hand moved right through the gargoyle. "Ah, right. Me… I'm the one not exactly real." Turning back to me, she continued to wear her excited smile. "But you've done it. Tell me how."

"It wasn't much," I admitted. "Simply willed it and told her to awaken."

"That's… strange." My aunt lost her smile, until looking back at Ebrill again. "And you? You must be excited to get back to your sisters, to join the fight."

Ebrill bit her lower lip, looking to me for help. "I don't exactly…"

"Her memory is coming back in pieces," I explained.

"You must find the Llyfr Sillafu, learn what spells you can—"

"Already one step ahead of you on that," I interrupted. "And actually, I've been able to sort of scan some of the pages, to see which ones are at my skill level, in a sense."

My aunt nodded, like she was proud of me, and said,

"Well then. Perhaps I fill you in on what I can while you finish your meal, then it's back to practicing."

"I would like that."

She looked us over, considering. "Perhaps it's best if I tell you only what is necessary, for now. I have seen glimpses of what is to come and know better than to spoil that future. What you need to know is that we are up against a great evil. It was contained for many years, but the bonds that held it are breaking. The dark magic is returning, although it can be harnessed by both sides—dark magic isn't inherently evil, but it has the power to easily corrupt."

"So, these attacks are coming because the doors are about to open?" I asked.

"It would seem that way."

"Can't we just go back and stop it somehow?"

"He has a point," Ebrill added. "He's been going back, affecting things. What if—"

"He will," my aunt cut in. "And it won't largely change things in the way you're thinking, but will make all the difference in the battle that is to come."

We spoke more on the subject, but mostly she filled us in on her travels to uncover the gargoyles. She had only gathered two so far, but there were papers in what she had passed on that included the right pieces, she believed —clues toward finding at least two more, along with other potential allies.

Soon, we were done. Ebrill and I tried for Kordelia again before training, but no luck. Since we were already on the rooftop, we figured that was as good a place as any to practice. I first went around and practiced my spell for the barrier wards, ensuring they were still up, then went over the spells I knew. Tarian for defensive boosts, which I found worked on Fatiha and Ebrill as well, and Elfenol Streic for the elemental strike.

"Try this," Fatiha said, breaking off a metal rod that was loose from the fence. It had likely gotten knocked free during last night's fighting. She tossed it over, and I caught it smoothly.

"As in…?"

"With the elemental strike."

I looked at the rod, said, "Elfenol Streic," and then twisted to go for fire and watched as the metal burst into flame. It was hot but didn't burn me, the spellcaster. With a pleased grin, I waved it around, only stopping when my gaze landed on the spot where the witch corpse had been earlier. "She's gone."

"Who?" my aunt asked.

"A witch's body," I explained.

Fatiha smiled, knowingly. "Something your aunt set up, wisely."

"Ah, yes." My aunt beamed with pride. "Nothing much, just a little spell that basically allows the house to absorb our enemies for its own power. As it strengthens the wards, it needs power. In this way, if we are attacked, we see benefits."

I laughed, not sure whether to be impressed or grossed out. Both worked. "You're saying… the house literally *eats* our enemies."

"Absorbs their energy," my aunt corrected, but then nodded. "But yes, basically. If someone is attacking us, it'll start the moment they are within the range of the spell—basically the grounds—although the more powerful they are, the slower the process."

"Unless they're dead," Fatiha added.

Ebrill was looking between the two, more excited as they spoke. "So, you're both... what, witches?"

"I was," my aunt replied, sending me a sensation like a punch to the chest.

"And me, not so much," Fatiha said.

"Wait, really?" I put a hand to my mouth. "Sorry, I didn't mean to sound so surprised, it's just that I figured..."

Fatiha gave me a forgiving smile. "I like to help. Do what I can without getting my hands dirty."

"So, you're like Tonto," I said. "Or... Alfred."

"You fancy yourself Batman, now?" Fatiha laughed. "Wow, you all seeing how fast that ego grows?"

My aunt's remnant chuckled.

"What's a Batman?" Ebrill asked.

"A superhero," I replied, but then thought about it. "Er, like a witch, but in this case, he uses fun gadgets instead of powers or magic."

"So, like a knight?"

Now it was my turn to laugh. "Yes, a dark knight. I'll show you sometime. For now," I turned back to my aunt, and held up my hand to bring up the screen with the spells I had scanned. "What are we thinking for next ones to try?"

"Are you seeing a gauge of your leveling?" Fatiha asked.

I nodded, looking at what I'd begun to think of as my XP bar. "Sure. But it doesn't seem to have gone up much since last time."

"Diminishing returns," my aunt said. "My guess is, once you start using your magic for real purposes—battle magic in a real battle, revealing spells and whatnot to actually reveal secrets, you will see jumps in your advancement."

"Ah, damn. I was kind of hoping I could cast my defense or ward spell over and over and watch those levels rack up, but yeah, that makes sense." Looking at my spells, I frowned. "Wait a minute, I don't have any attack spells yet, other than the elemental strike."

"Which counts, but yes." My aunt flashed out and then appeared next to me, apparently able to see my screens, as she started scrolling. "There—'Hurtio.'" She indicated the spell, which showed a simple motion of thrusting my hand forward.

"It... hurts them?" I asked, humored.

"Stuns, actually. At your level, it's probably the best 'attack' spell you're going to get."

I tried it but couldn't tell if it worked.

"Try on me," Fatiha offered.

Before I had a chance to reply, Ebrill stepped in front of her. "No, I can take more. In case it does hurt, try it on me first."

Oddly, the look in her eyes made me think she might enjoy it if the spell did hurt.

"It won't cause any damage," my aunt said again.

Ebrill shrugged. "In case."

I chuckled and thrust out my hand, saying, "Hurtio."

Sure enough, a gust of wind seemed to hit Ebrill and for a moment she was unable to move. It only lasted about a second and then she shook it off and looking at me, impressed.

"Hit them with that, then a strike from that fire baton of yours, and I think we have something."

"Not a baton," I said, eying the fence pole. One end of it was sharp, so I could definitely see it being a useful tool. "But, yeah."

"And your education?" my aunt asked.

"What?"

"I want to know your plans for college."

I looked at Fatiha and Ebrill for help here, but both were watching me with curiosity.

"Sorry, but all of this seems more important," I pointed out. "Why is school even being discussed?"

"Your aunt has a good point," Fatiha said. "This fighting, uncovering secrets, learning more about Ebrill and her friends might all be the priority, but it isn't your entire life. It's not going to take up all of your time."

I frowned, then looked at Ebrill as my mind wandered to some different ways she could use up my time. Then again, maybe they had a point. Fighting and fucking sounded great, but I had to wonder if it would pay the bills.

"Wait a sec." I turned to my aunt and Fatiha. "Aren't we set for money? What exactly would be the point of college? Surely, I'm not going to go get some desk job, after."

"You'll be taken care of," my aunt said. "But you have to be smart about it. Have a cover. Spend your time studying matters that will help, and that will keep you prepared to do great things during times of peace, as well. Assuming we have those at some point."

"This war has been going on for far too long," Ebrill said.

Fatiha nodded. "Although you have been out, so in fairness we should say the war portion of it only happens whenever one side is growing close to the Liahona."

"Is that so?"

"On that note, is someone going to tell me more about this thing anytime soon?" I faced my aunt, waiting.

She nodded. "From what I've been able to learn… and Ebrill, you might have recalled more by this point?" At a shake of Ebrill's head, my aunt continued. "Very well. From what I understand, it's like a key. It opens an access point."

"To where?"

"Not to where, exactly… To what. Like a vault, in a sense. A vault of power—magic we can't dream of. Magic…"

"All speculation," Ebrill interrupted.

"So, you do remember?" Fatiha asked.

Ebrill nodded, slowly. "Bits of it, yes. I remember someone wanted to get their hands on it, and that we couldn't let them." Her eyes narrowed, looking intently at each of us in turn, my aunt, then Fatiha. Finally, me. "How do I know you all… I mean—"

"That we're on the right side of all this?" I asked. "Easy. You know me."

"Not well."

"Enough.

"Suffice it to say," my aunt interjected, "that we're not your enemy. Your enemy, whomever it was, likely died long ago."

"Or maybe all sides are the enemy, now, and I've been brought back to put an end to it. To ensure nobody ever gets their hands on the Liahona."

"Ebrill… that's not the case." I stepped toward her,

hand up, but she pulled away. "I promise you, we're in this together."

She was crouched now, as if ready to pounce. As wrong as it was, the sound of an attack actually came as a relief. Nothing like having a common enemy to bring two sides together. An explosion rocked the side of the house, followed by a ball of fire tearing through our magical barriers and exploding on Kordelia's statue.

One nod from Ebrill, and I knew we were good at least until this was over. Somehow, the enemy had broken through our wards. We needed to find out how, then stop them.

# 13

"Tell me how they got through the wards," I shouted, already trying to cast new ones, indicating Kordelia's statue.

My aunt moved her hands and spoke in what sounded like gibberish but in my head came through as, "Obliterate them." Nothing happened, as I had figured would be the case. She wasn't real, exactly, so her spells wouldn't work. She had apparently forgotten that little fact.

"What worries me more is that this happened *after* the house absorbed the fallen witch," Fatiha said, charging over to the hatch to head down. "Meaning something strong is out there, and we'd better get into hiding."

I took a step to follow, but Ebrill's eyes showed fright and worry as they darted between the way down and Kordelia's statue. Clearly, she was torn about leaving it unprotected. This was, after all, a woman she greatly cared about, even if she was now made of stone. Here I was trying to earn her trust, so the last thing I could do was run and leave the statue—and therefore the woman she could in theory become—to be destroyed by whatever monsters were sending magic at us.

"Jericho, you're not strong enough," Fatiha said.

My aunt flittered to the edge of the roof and gasped. "They have a Drow."

"A what?" I asked, racking my brain for what that meant. It hit, then, from some old game my friend had played. "A dark elf?"

"Those who were left behind," she replied, nodding, a fireball passing through her to hit Kordelia again. "When the world changed, when magic left our lands—they went to live below the surface, uprooting evil and unleashing demons that had slept for millennia before their arrival. To think that they're involved…" Her eyes went to Ebrill. "You'd better hope we wake Kordelia soon, or there won't be a Kordelia to wake."

"We can't let that happen," Ebrill said, moving toward the ledge, hand held up with a glowing light coming from it.

"You'd take them all on yourself?" My aunt appeared directly in her path. "We can't lose you, and with what they likely have down there… I don't think you'd make it."

Ebrill bared her teeth, growling.

Another fireball was incoming, the worry from Ebrill palpable. If I could do anything for her, I would, and that included stopping this onslaught on her friend.

Digging deep, I was pretty sure I had found a way. I didn't want to say anything and get their hopes up, plus, there was no time to spare. Eyes closed, going to that spot within where all of the crazy magic had come from over the years, I focused on the outside force, then on us and protecting Kordelia.

A shifting of stone caused me to open my eyes, but I didn't break focus. Good thing, too, because as I watched, my transmutation magic was moving the building, changing it. Stones were gathering up in a defensive wall, moving like tiles clicking into place even as the rooftop lowered. Everyone turned to me, but I kept my attention on what was happening. A moment later, even the metal of the garden gates and vines were forming barriers around Kordelia, as best as they could.

"You're destroying my house," my aunt said, but it was in awe, not anger.

"And protecting Kordelia," Ebrill added, running to my side. She kissed my cheek and wrapped her arms around me. The effect was an instant surge in power, so that the stone and bricks and metal started merging together while attacks began to hit in rapid succession from below.

"Don't let go," I said, and closed my eyes again, feeling the heat of her body against me, embracing the power as it flowed through my limbs and out into the building.

There was more, too—it was like I could see through the walls of the building, sense vibrations and even breaths. A group of witches was attempting to break through at the rear of the house, led by one of those dark elves. With a deep breath, I made the earth come alive, turning dirt and stone into golems that rose above our enemy and assaulted them. I tripped them with vines and brought tree limbs down upon them. They tried to send attacks at the trees and golems but had nothing that could stop my attack.

Two witches broke for it, running for the rear entrance of the house and casting spells as they ran, buffers that gave them defense and protective shields. Not enough, though, because as soon as they smashed through the door, I opened up the ground and swallowed them into it before closing it on them.

Screams became muffled whimpers that vibrated through my skull, then were gone.

"How are you doing this?" my aunt asked, and I sensed her moving about the house, watching through the windows as the fight continued.

"It's all that makes sense," I replied, and caused a ripple effect in the earth, attempting to swallow one of the dark elves as well, but she turned, leaped, and was gone.

At her retreat, others began to flee as well, so that in a matter of less than a minute, the assault was completely thwarted.

I fell out of the spell and would have collapsed to my knees if not for Ebrill catching me and helping me to stand.

She took me by the chin, stared into my eyes, and said, "Thank you." Then her lips were on mine, tongue testing the waters, and her kiss filled me with energy. Not enough to fully stand, but at least enough to kiss her back.

"That was… something," my aunt said as she returned to our side, ignoring the kiss.

"Do you plan on restoring it?" Fatiha asked, glancing around.

I looked now, too, and saw that the roof, once flat with the garden and rails, was now curved, leading to the main defensive spot around Kordelia's statue. It basically put her into a sort of a tomb, accessible from our side.

"This might be best," I said. "At least, until we know they don't plan on attacking again any time soon." Next, I cast new protective wards, figuring it couldn't hurt, and nodded to the way down.

"Seriously, though..." My aunt motioned to our surroundings. "This was impressive. If they bring a stronger force, we might need to do it again, but... with more."

"Like a magic version of *Home Alone*?" I asked.

She cocked her head, then laughed. "Yes, I suppose you could say that."

"I'll have to nod and smile while pretending like I know what you are talking about," Ebrill said, doing just that.

"I'll catch you up when this is over," I promised. "Or before, if there's time."

"Might be hard, since I don't own any televisions," my aunt said.

I guffawed, then thought of something. "But... since you left money and the house to us, that's something we can fix, right?"

She smiled, then nodded. "If you feel it's necessary."

"Maybe not right away. But... yes." I turned back to Kordelia, raising a hand. "For now, let's see if there's any way I can wake her. I'm feeling the power burning bright, so..." But no, nothing. "So..." I scrunched my nose into a glare, turned from it, and kept walking.

"We're going to need her," Ebrill said. "I... feel it."

"What if..." I analyzed Ebrill, wondering if she knew where the Liahona was.

"Say it."

"Well, maybe we need the Liahona to awaken her."

Ebrill pursed her lips, then shook her head. "Not something I can accept right now. We'll find a way."

Seeing that pushing the subject wasn't the smart move, I nodded. "Whatever you think is best, I'll be here at your side."

"That so?"

"I promise."

She gave me a sidelong glance, then allowed a hint of a smile. "Maybe you should get some rest."

"I can keep going."

"I'm sure you can." She ran her tongue along her upper lip, turning her head so Fatiha wouldn't see. "But some sleep might help you, and who knows when the next attack might come."

"We'll wake you, if the explosions don't," Fatiha offered. "Go on, do as she says."

"Sure." I nodded, then started for the stairs. "Oh, Ebrill, maybe you can tag along. I wanted to tell you more about that dream."

"Of course."

She came with me, earning a suspicious but humored glance from Fatiha, and soon the two of us were back in my room. Ebrill squeezed my hand as she gestured to the bed.

"Go on."

"Oh?" I glanced at the bed, then her, and started to undress. First my shirt, then I glanced her way as I started to undo my pants.

"You're… going to sleep nude?"

I froze. "Wait, I thought… isn't that why you winked? Why you wanted to come up here with me?"

Her eyes went wide, and she cocked her head. "Honestly, I was thinking you could sleep again, find out about seeing me again, like before. But… would that help you sleep?"

Choosing my words carefully, here, I said, "I'm a bit wound up. A tension release?"

"That's how you proposition a lady?" She laughed, stepped over, and began helping me with the pants. "Maybe just a massage."

"A massage?"

She nodded, her hand slipping into my boxer briefs to grab my stiff cock and slowly caress it. "What, you don't like my massage?"

I closed my eyes, feeling her hand on my shaft, then opened them to see her pulling my boxer briefs down and watched as she stroked my cock. Then she guided me to the bed, grabbed a box of tissues, and had me lie on my back as she stroked me with both hands, rocking with the motion.

"You're sure you don't want…?" My eyes roamed down, hands on her legs.

She shook her head. "When we're ready."

I relaxed, letting the moment happen. Her firm grip brought me to release, her eyes watching me hungrily as I came. She wiped me clean with the tissues, then lay down next to me, one leg draped over my cock, arm over my side exactly as we had been the night before.

"There, I hope that helps you sleep."

My mind filled with fantasies of her going down on me, of the two of us on a hillside fucking under the moonlight, and I moaned, the shivers of an orgasmic aftershock running through me as my eyes started to close.

# 14

I was there again, in that little hut, but the women were gone. I stood there all by myself, staring at a small sculpture of a gargoyle. Clay, it seemed, fairly crude, and not like the sexy ones Ebrill and her friend had proven to be. In fact, this one was more like a cross between them and the Okinawan lion statues out front of my aunt's house. It got me thinking, wondering if those statues could somehow come to life. But it also got me wondering what these elves, if that's what they were, knew about gargoyles.

For the first time, I considered that maybe they weren't elves at all, simply gargoyles if gargoyles didn't turn to stone during the day. Wherever I was, could it be possible that these ones turned into the women I had seen last time?

The rest of the room wasn't anything special. Wood floors and beams overhead, a trunk with clothing, and some paper under a bodice that had been tossed aside. I took a step closer to the paper, lifting the bodice at the sight of swirling patterns. These patterns… I recognized them. In fact, even the writing looked familiar.

On a hunch, I held up my hand to see if I could access my screen from here. Sure enough, it popped up and let me access the pages I had scanned from the *Llyfr Sillafu*, the spell book. Only, these ones weren't complete. It was like they were copying it over, or possibly even creating it.

Could these women—elves, gargoyles, or otherwise—be the ones who created the spell book?

Voices sounded from the main entrance, and they weren't friendly. One was the goblin with the snake eyes from before, I was sure of it. Another was the deeper, terrifying voice. I snuck to the back of the hut, about to make my escape, when I saw a stream nearby. It wasn't the stream that caught my attention, but an elf… the one I now knew was Ebrill, somehow before she became a gargoyle, if that made any sense.

One way I could tell she wasn't really a gargoyle here was that the sun was shining on her nude form, her back to me, water dripping down her round ass as she bathed herself. She started to turn, looking up at something, the underside of her breast exposed. I told myself to look away, tried even, but damn, that was impossible. You don't see beauty like that and avert your eyes.

The voices reminded me that danger was coming, and I knew that if they caught her there like that, she would be in serious trouble. Realizing I only had one move here, I darted out, staying low as I sprinted toward her.

*Shit, shit, shit*, my mind was saying, while my mouth moved as I tried to think about how to warn her. In an instant, she turned, fully exposed and facing me, and a figure rose from my left as a shout came and motion of hands.

A force knocked me sideways. My ears rang. Two women moved up on me. One had red hair, the other black, and green light emitted from one of their hands in a way that made me wonder if I would live to see the next few seconds.

"Enemy… coming…" I managed to get out, hands up as I knelt. "I'm on your side."

"You again," I heard from one side, and then they had me, all of us running.

"Grab your damn clothes!" the other sort of hissed and shouted at Ebrill, who still stood there nude, staring in confusion. At those words, though, she snapped into action, running from the water and going for a dress nearby.

Only, there wasn't time to dress, so she ran with us, clutching the garment to her chest and eyeing me with confusion.

"You two, that way," one of the others said, and then they broke left. We darted right, going along the curve of the hill. I glanced back to see the forms of one horned man and one shorter figure. that I took to be the goblin from before, but really had no idea.

"Get down," Ebrill hissed, pulling me with her so that we slid down the grassy hill, out of sight. As she started to pull the dress on to cover herself, she glared at me. "Avert your gaze."

"Sorry, I…" I turned, thinking I would peek to ensure that we weren't being followed. "Will they be okay?"

"They can handle themselves," she said, and clucked

her tongue, motioning me to follow now that she was dressed.

She guided me along a ledge, the two of us leaping down. We ran in a crouch, stopping at a grouping of trees. There in hiding, pressed together to avoid being caught, we stared into each other's eyes.

"Who are you, sir, and why do you look at me like that?" Ebrill whispered.

"I..." No answer came to mind, only the intense need to lean forward and kiss her. Our lips met, her eyes wide, but then they closed as she got into it, tongue in my mouth, hands moving along my arms.

She pulled back. "What sorcery is this?"

"None," I replied. "Other than your beauty pulling me, leaving me with little or no will of my own." Her scoff was accompanied by an eye roll, making me wonder if what I'd said had really been *that* bad. It didn't matter though, because it was true. "My name is Jericho."

Her hands, I noted, were still on my arms. The mocking in her eyes faded to curiosity again. "Very well, Jericho. Would you mind explaining what you were doing with the likes of them?"

"I wasn't. I had just come out of the shed and spotted you bathing when they arrived."

Now her hands pulled back. "You were watching me?"

"No. Not like that."

"You weren't watching me?"

"I mean, I didn't mean to. But there was the threat, and then they—"

A hand on my leg. A smile. "It's nothing to worry about, as long as you... liked what you saw."

I gulped and then blinked, remembering where we

were. “And those two? The goblin-looking one and the other, who are they?”

“Danger,” she replied, fingers moving up my leg. “Are you afraid?”

“Never,” I lied, although the answer was a tricky one—at the moment, I was more afraid she would pull her hand away than anything else.

“Good, because there’s no need to be. I have you.” Her hand went for my zipper, but she stared at it in confusion. “Are you a priest?”

“What?”

“This chastity belt, it’s—”

I caught her meaning and unzipped my pants for her. “Not a chastity belt. Just, something we use where I’m from. Easy access.”

“Easy… access.” She bit her lip to keep from laughing, then indicated that I should kneel as she pulled my pants and underwear down.

Still amped up from running and not totally sure what was happening, I wasn’t exactly hard yet, but not fully limp. The result was that it appeared I was quite well endowed, and the arch in her eyebrow showed she noticed.

“Now you’ve seen mine, and I’ve seen yours,” she said. “We’re even.”

“We’re what?”

“Go ahead, put that monstrosity away.” There was a hint of a smile to her lips, but she was already turning away, scanning the area for trouble.

“You can’t be serious.”

“I’m sorry, Jericho, but what did you expect? That I would let you take me right here on death’s doorstep?”

She shook her head with a chuckle. "Where you're from, the women must be something else, indeed, if that's how they behave."

"Well…" My mind went to the future, to the gargoyle her, and I pursed my lips, to stop from saying anything. 'Something else' was right.

I tucked myself away, kind of annoyed by the whole situation, then leaned over to look out at the grassy field and hills beyond. The scent in the air reminded me of honeysuckle, the warm breeze pleasant compared to the humidity of D.C. Having only the night before received a hand job from the future version of this lady, the whole scenario with 'showing her mine' didn't leave me so embarrassed, although technically this had been *this* Ebrill's first experience with me in that way.

Glancing over at her, I had to know. "Are you, I mean… do you ever change form?"

Her eyes narrowed as they darted over. "I'm no shifter."

"Even at night?"

She shook her head, confused. "Do you?"

I chuckled. "No."

"I have to assume you know some who do, or you wouldn't be asking such a ridiculous question."

"In a sense, yes."

"You seem… decent." Her eyes lingered on me, weighing. "And yet, you saved me. Or, helped me, anyway, while sneaking a peek."

I laughed. "Come on, we're even. You said so."

"Fair enough. But with your strange style of dress, your odd… accent? You don't belong here, that's plain to see. Tell me."

"You'll find out more, eventually. The easy version is, I think I'm here to help you, somehow."

"And how would you help me, exactly? Are you a mage?"

"In training."

She nodded, eyes moving over me. "But not strong enough to take the likes of those two on, or we wouldn't have run."

"Not yet," I agreed. "Although I have a good trainer."

"Here they come," Ebrill said. "Kordelia and Aerona. Act natural, and keep your cock in your pants this time."

"That's not fair," I started, only to feel a splitting headache, followed by everything going blurry.

"Are you feeling well?" she asked and then frowned, eyes roaming over me as I started to fade.

A jolt hit, and then I was back in my room in my aunt's house.

Ebrill hadn't left my side—gargoyle Ebrill, that is. As soon as our eyes met, it was clear that she remembered everything that had happened. She was on me in a second, lips pressed against mine, tongue jutting out and toying with my tongue. Her hands moved along my chest and then down, cupping my balls and pulling my hands to her breasts.

You better believe I was into it every bit as much as she was. I moved her armor aside and took her breasts in my hands, playing with her nipples, and then moved from her mouth to take one of those nipples with my lips and nibble on it. I reached down and brushed against the inside of her thigh, about to push her loincloth aside, when a warning went off in my head.

She cringed, apparently feeling it too.

"The wards," I said, cock throbbing and gut clenching at the thought of stopping now.

Ebrill met my gaze and shook her head. "Fuck it, right? The wards might hold. They should, and we can be fast."

Again, the shooting warning, this time so hard it was painful.

Fatiha appeared at the doorway, clearly expecting to find us exactly like this, and motioned. "No time for that. They're breaking through."

"How long have they been attacking?" Ebrill asked.

"First strike."

We all shared a look of horror. Then Ebrill and I were up and dressing before running to follow Fatiha to the rooftop. Halfway there, however, the house shook as explosions sounded, and a wall in the room visible down the hall and to the right suddenly crumbled.

"Shit," I shouted, motioning them away from that direction.

"Kordelia," Ebrill said, pulling my arm back. "We can't leave her up there, we can't just..."

"We won't," I said, and shouted for Fatiha, who was already moving. "We need to go to the rooftop. Defend from there."

"It's too exposed!" she countered.

"We have no choice."

She saw the determination in our eyes, grunted, and motioned for us to follow her to the roof.

# 15

"Do what you did before," Fatiha said, leading us up.

I paused, though, hand on the wall. "Why do I need to go to the roof to do it?"

She blinked, then nodded. "You can do it from here?"

"More than likely." I glanced over at Ebrill, who was eyeing me with interest. The words I was about to say could be taken wrong, but I was starting to feel comfortable enough around her that I didn't have a problem telling her what I was thinking. "Before, when you were close, my powers seemed to surge. Especially when you kissed my cheek."

"You want me to kiss your cheek before you start?" Ebrill smirked. "I can do that."

With a purse of my lips, I shook my head. "Maybe we should head back to the room."

"Jericho!" Fatiha chided, folding her arms. "We're under attack, I hope you aren't using this as an opportunity to… well, you know."

I shook my head, all business. "As dumb as it sounds... I felt a difference."

"Maybe because of my magical past," Ebrill offered. She was already walking with me, taking my hand in the process to pull me along. The energy soared, and I gave Fatiha a look of excitement. To my surprise, she appeared bothered. Jealous?

Whatever it was, the moment passed, and she called after us, "I'll just be... hoping it all works out okay. From the... where should I go?"

"With us," I said over my shoulder.

Ebrill stopped and turned to me. "Wait, you really are serious. Because I'm pretty sure her being in the room will keep us... at least partially decent."

I nodded, then started walking again as Fatiha caught up. As much as I would have loved to continue what Ebrill and I had started, this was clearly not the time. That said, her little assumption that we couldn't do much with Fatiha in the room made my mind wander... and fill with images of the two of us fucking like rabbits while the older woman watched. Fatiha wasn't so old, anyway. Much older than me, sure, but even with her silver hair, I could easily see her hanging out with my mom, sipping wine and being all proper. If my mom had been into that sort of thing, anyway.

Still, I glanced over at Fatiha and the thought of it gave me the tingles. She was beautiful, in an older, elegant way. When she saw me looking, her eyes narrowed—not in a frown, but in a playful, curious way.

Explosions from outside, along with the walls shaking, reminded me why this wasn't the time for such thoughts.

I turned back to the door, which we had reached, and

held it open for the ladies. As soon as we were in, swirling darkness visible outside the window, Ebrill wasted no time wrapping her arms around me.

"Would it help if she tried, too?" Ebrill asked, glancing over at Fatiha, who had been about to sit but froze mid-way.

My mind instantly went to thoughts of this being a trap, but when she motioned Fatiha over and the older woman didn't fight it, instead embracing me from the opposite side of Ebrill, I blinked, blood rushing to my groin.

"This will be less awkward if we lie down," I said, and moved for the bed, quickly tucking my rising erection under my waistband so it wouldn't be noticeable.

"Less awkward?" Fatiha asked, but she shared a look of curiosity with Ebrill, and then they both joined me.

"Maybe skin on skin would help," Ebrill offered. I thought they were teasing me. But their hands moved under my shirt and found my chest.

"It's imperative you find that Liahona," Fatiha said, her mouth next to my ear. "You'll need it to wake Kordelia, and I don't think this house can take much more."

Ebrill seemed less certain, but said, "Fight them off, make sure we're safe, then… we try. Go to the dream, do whatever you can—I think that's the answer."

With a nod, I lay back, closed my eyes, and focused.

One might think two women lying in bed with their hands on my chest, one moving slowly toward my abs, would be distracting. Instead, this was what somehow fueled my power, unleashing floodgates of energy that I pushed into my transmutation magic.

As I started to merge with the house, one of their

hands moved south, causing a jolt of energy to run through me. Then the fingers were on my shaft, a moment later gripping my stiffening cock, and I was gone.

Again, I was the house.

Not sure why this intimate act amped up my power, but fully embracing it, I let my consciousness loose to run through the house freely. The attack was indeed at the next level, confirming what Fatiha had said. If we didn't end this soon, we could be in serious trouble. As witches and demons attacked the house with spells and some dug in, searching for other ways, something long and monstrous moved in the darkness, surrounding the house like a serpent of the night.

While they weren't in, I wasn't sure what my options were until the dark form moved to the front, about to attack. It hesitated, giving me what I needed to understand. The *shisa* statues out front gave off an interesting energy, so I moved into them to see what could be done.

As I hoped, the *shisa* both came alive, breaking free as Ebrill had, to reveal two dragon-like lions. Not large, but formidable. Their strength radiated off them, the hidden power of protectors pushing them to charge for the shape in the darkness.

They connected, throwing themselves at the beast so that it convulsed and surged back at them, wrapping around and revealing itself to be a serpent like a Chinese dragon, green bursts of energy shooting out of it like lightning bolts. The *shisa* moved fast to dodge and attack as I did what I could to contain the serpent with roots and flying rocks.

Others amongst the enemy realized what was happening and moved in to join the fight, while a side group managed to get past the wards and into a back entrance of the house. I brought down part of the first floor to crush them, quickly replacing it as the house rumbled. Two managed to push themselves free, red auras glowing and seemingly unharmed.

They shouted threats, but already I had the *shisa* charging away from the serpent, using my power to raise the ground as barricades to keep it out while the *shisa* dealt with those already in.

If the *shisa* could come to life, why not more? Thinking outside the box, I focused on the floors and walls, feeling them morph into humanoid forms that met my enemy in battle. With each push of my power, surges like electricity charged through me to let me know I was getting stronger, better.

Another level increase was coming soon, I could sense it. Two demons met my floor golems in battle. While I took down one by smashing it to blood and pulp, the second demon hit my golems with a fist of vibrating red energy that caused them to shatter at its touch. It seemed to look at me, and I felt its presence inside me, pulsating as if that red energy were going to rip me to shreds.

I pushed back, reaching deeper within and working to bring whatever I could rally in my arsenal to destroy him. The *shisa* was there, tearing through his leg and then dodging again as the serpent nearly got it, and then I had my focus back. With a surge of energy, I brought wire from the wall, vaguely aware of electricity going off in certain rooms while I zapped the fucker and pulled him into the wall, closing it back up.

More figures appeared, some that I was able to pull into the walls. Others were too strong though, and used their magic to push back and resist. Rumbling sounded, then shaking.

"It's not enough," a voice said, and suddenly I was pulled from my focus, back to the room where I lay with them, both now propping themselves up.

I saw why, too. Lines formed in the walls, splitting, some even showing hints of magic cracking through. As much as I was achieving, the outside forces were too much for me.

"Leave me in there, I can—"

"No," Fatiha said, already moving for the door. "We get to the panic room, hold in there. More than anything, we'll need the Liahona."

Ebrill joined me, my hand on her lower back, guiding her, as we followed Fatiha through the door. I wasn't as sure as the older woman and Ebrill looked skeptical, but I hadn't been doing this long, so I didn't really know. Ebrill had been out of commission for so long that listening to Fatiha seemed the best move.

As we moved through the hall, though, listening to the rumbling throughout the building and a new roaring from outside, Ebrill whispered, "It's not going to hold," and then she shouted for Kordelia as part of a nearby wall crumbled in.

Two lanky red demons with long claws and horns charged in. Ebrill felled the first with a flash of claws. I hit the second with a "Hurtio" stunning spell, then an icy fist thanks to my elemental strike. Apparently, I had left the metal from the fence in the room, but it was too late to get it, now. She finished off the bastard, hitting it where my ice had frozen its jaw so that the demon's head shattered. My level went up again. I quickly adjusted the attributes with the points available, even though I knew this was all somewhat arbitrary, considering it was essentially my transmutational magic giving me a way to regulate my power advancement. When I was done, it read:

***Level 2 ~~Witch~~ MAGE***

***Statistics***
***Strength: 6***
***Defense: 6***
***Speed: 6***
***Luck: 7***
***Charisma: 6***

***Mana: 320***

***Current Spells***
***Passive: Situational Alchemy, AKA "Transmutation"***
***Active: Ddiogelu (protection ward), Elfenol Streic (elemental strike), Tarian (defense boost), Hurtio (stun).***

"KEEP USING those spells every chance you get," Ebrill said, and I nodded as I cast the "Tarian" defensive boost on all of us.

"Quickly," Fatiha shouted, and we charged after her.

More rumbling, and the dark form of the serpent crashed through part of the house, cutting off the hall as the walls collapsed and some of the floor gave out. Fatiha turned toward us, eyes wide, when more of the ceiling fell between us.

I jumped back, grabbing Ebrill and pulling her close. For a moment, the house continued to shake. We turned toward the door to our left and took a step, when it opened to reveal Steph.

"Stay back," I said, hand out, ready to cast a stun spell her way.

Steph stood there, lifted a hand, and her death knights appeared behind her—three of them, at least, that we could see.

"Wait." Ebrill leaped forward, hands on Steph's head. For a moment, I thought she was going to suck the life out of my ex. Instead, a darkness floated away like smoke, leaving Steph without the death knights, confusion in her eyes… and then tears.

"Oh, no," Steph said. "No, no, no…"

"Steph?"

She turned to me, hands on Ebrill's, guiding them down. "It's me. The real me, this time."

# 16

"I don't... understand," I admitted, sounds of roaring and the shaking building around us as I stared at Steph, no more malice in her eyes.

"Maybe I can help with that." Ebrill turned to me. "It was a curse. They're sort of my specialty, and I instantly recognized the one on her."

"She was cursed?" I took a step toward them, very confused about not only the situation but how I should react. I'd been fairly intimate with Ebrill, while assuming Steph was trying to kill me. Well, she was, but because she was cursed. "Steph, was that before or after... us?"

Steph's cheeks went red and she bit her lower lip. "I don't remember, exactly. I mean, I remember us, of course —how could I not? But... when the curse—"

Her sentence was cut off as Ebrill put a hand on her again. This time, the gargoyle's eyes went purple momentarily, then she withdrew her hand. "Better?"

"It's all..." Steph put a hand to her mouth. "Oh, God. There was this woman, she came to me and I remember her sitting with me in a coffee shop. I thought it was weird that she was talking to me at all, but then the barista came over with two macchiatos, and when she offered one to me it looked so delicious. But," she turned to Ebrill, "what, she drugged me?"

"Maybe? More than likely, to get you somewhere secluded where she could then perform the real curse on you. An alley, a—"

"Car, yes. It's all coming back." Steph's eyes were wide with sorrow and horror as she remembered.

"So, the death knights, those weren't you, either?" I asked.

"The wraith knights?" she asked. "Those are mine, as is my magic. But I was coming to find you at your aunt's beckoning. Gertrude called to me and… oh, no, no. It's all coming back."

"You killed her," I said, nodding solemnly.

She eyed me, then slowly shook her head. "I… No. I didn't."

"Well maybe not you, but those others you were with."

"Not us."

I frowned, confused, noticing how her eyes had moved past me, widening. If she was about to accuse Ebrill, I was going to have to call bullshit. The gargoyle had been stone, only woken by my touch. But when I turned around, it wasn't Ebrill that Steph was looking at. Fatiha stood there. Dust from fallen debris covered her sweat-soaked forehead, and her hair looked wild. It was her eyes that caught my attention, though, because they were filled with hatred as she stared at Steph.

"What's she doing in here?" Fatiha hissed. "She's evil."

"Not anymore," Steph replied, taking a step back. "And that was only because of you. Jericho, this is the woman."

"It can't be..." I shook my head, not accepting it.

"She was the one. In the coffee shop, and... after. I'll never forget that face."

"Jericho, this is ridiculous." Fatiha took a step forward, hands out. "We were cuddling, lying in bed with my hand on your manhood and you—"

"She what?" Steph asked, and then looked at Ebrill with narrowed eyes, as if waiting for her confession next.

"To be honest, I didn't know it was *her* hand," I said.

"The point is," Fatiha continued, "how can you doubt me right now, after what we've shared?"

My eyes met Ebrill's, and that was enough. If she said she had broken a curse on Steph, I believed her. Which meant that I wasn't sure I could believe Fatiha. There was only one way to find out, as far as I was concerned. One thing I could say that would be the ultimate test.

"We'll all leave here, together. Leave this all behind... and abandon the search for the Liahona."

As I'd expected but hoped wouldn't be the case, Fatiha's reaction spelled out her position. While Ebrill looked confused and Steph relieved, Fatiha's eyes flashed with fury.

"You can't!" she shouted, stepping toward me, hand up and moving in a pattern I hadn't seen yet. "I trained you for this. Taught you how to harness the magic your aunt left behind, and now you want to waste it?"

"I'm not wasting it. I'm saying that if the item is gone, maybe that's for the best. The enemy sure seems to want it, so we should leave it hidden."

"No."

"No?" Ebrill stepped up next to me, staring intently at Fatiha.

"Don't you start!" Fatiha turned on her. "You weren't supposed to come back. That wasn't part of the plan. Keep your trap shut." Turning back to me, she finished with a movement of her hand and said, "I didn't want to do this, but since you give me no choice. Gorffwys!"

As she spoke the word, my mind went into a daze, the house and all gone, me back with the elf version of Ebrill. She spun to see me, eyes wide as she held a leg of what looked like chicken to her mouth.

It only lasted a moment, not even long enough for her to set the chicken leg down, and then I was back as a shout sounded. Steph was there, shoving Fatiha with both hands so that the older woman went flying into the wall and slammed her head against it, crumpling to the floor. Fatiha shrieked in pain, then turned, pointed a finger at Steph and opened her mouth to cast a curse. But suddenly one of the *shisas* came charging in, snapping her hand clean off and then turning to her as blood fell from its lips. Damn, if it hadn't been on my side that would've been terrifying.

The other *shisa* followed, when another section of the building tore out and the serpent appeared, mouth open and consumed the *shisa* in one bite. It spun around, coming back for us as Ebrill grabbed me and pulled me with her.

"Steph, was it?" Ebrill shouted. "You want to live, run!"

Steph was with us a moment later, wild eyes taking this all in, the surviving *shisa* at her side. A look of sorrow was in the *shisa's* large eyes, causing Steph to pat its head as we ran.

"This is really happening?" I asked, shaking my head as I tried to comprehend everything. "You didn't kill my aunt, but the woman I thought was her servant and was helping me did, and she had laid a curse on you. So, my girlfriend is innocent of that but has been under a curse to get me here and attack me, in a strange way, and… I kind of cheated on her."

Ebrill scoffed, but Steph glanced at her and shrugged. "Since I wasn't really myself, I'd say we can ignore that little part. Start over."

"So, you're not my girlfriend?"

"Would you want her to be?" Ebrill asked.

Turning to look at the stunning beauty that was this gargoyle woman, I was at a loss for words. With a shrug, I finally blurted out, "I have no idea what's going on. I'm just trying to keep my head above water."

She guffawed, but then smiled as I led the way to the roof. "We're going for her?"

"Of course," I replied. "If they're going to take this place down, we at least have to protect Kordelia."

"What about the others?" Steph asked as we went, more rumbling and explosions sounding muffled.

"Others?" I asked.

"The rest of the gargoyles. I remember bits of what I overheard when under her influence, and there was talk of five in all."

"Five of us?" Ebrill blinked, shook her head, and laughed. "Now this memory loss bit is starting to agitate me. All we know about is the one on the roof. Kordelia."

"It's possible my aunt never found the rest," I admitted.

"Or that she never shared their location."

"For now, the one." I reached the ladder and climbed up, pushing through to the rooftop.

I reached down for Steph's hand to help her up, when her eyes turned red and her hair turned white and flowed out behind her. My life was forfeit in that moment, I was sure of it, but her death wraiths appeared and lunged past me, followed by the sickening sounds of blades on flesh. By the time I managed to spin and take a look, they already had three attacking demons on the ground, while one fell over the side of the roof, cleaved in two.

"Nice work," I said, helping Steph up the rest of the way.

"Don't try to pretend that you didn't doubt me," she said with a laugh, her voice sounding slightly off while her body was in this form, with her eyes still red. Apparently, this was a power of hers when not under the curse.

"Where'd you get that power?" I asked.

She arched an eyebrow while turning to thrust out a fireball as a short goblin climbed over the edge of the roof. It dodged and came back up, only to have its head chopped halfway down by a death wraith.

"Maybe that's a conversation for another time," I admitted.

"You think?"

Now it was my turn, casting "Tarian" to boost us and "Hurtio" to stun one of two witches who made it up to join the assault. Three strange flying beasts came from the sky, but Ebrill was up now and rose to meet the first two, tearing them down and pummeling them. Once they were on the roof, I was able to get a good look at the bat-like creatures with their eerily humanoid faces.

"Vampires?"

Steph scoffed. "Not even close. Vampires are hot."

"Oh?"

"I mean, nothing compared to you, of course." She grimaced, shooting off more fireballs. "Am I… I mean," summoning two more death wraiths to charge at a wind golem, "am I supposed to say things like that?"

"Our situation is a bit murky, what with you trying to kill me before."

"Right after going down on you, I have to point out." She spun and attacked again, this time hitting a winged beast right out of the sky. "And again, curse."

"Wait, so… you were cursed to go down on me?" I caught a flying beast with a stun spell, watching as it face-planted into the railing and flipped over, then fell over the edge. Two more hit me from behind, tackling me to the roof. Ebrill swooped in to take care of one, but a demon caught her from the other side while another flying beast joined the assault on me.

"Elfenol Streic," I shouted, turning my fist to go with fire, and hit the first one square on the nose. As it fell back in a ball of flames, it hit the other one with it, which caught fire, too. I noticed that my level increased again! I made quick adjustments, knowing this wasn't the best time, but now the screen read:

***Level 3 MAGE***

***Statistics***

***Strength: 9***

***Defense: 8***

***Speed: 8***
***Luck: 7***
***Charisma: 7***

***Mana: 350***

***Current Spells***
***Passive: Situational Alchemy, AKA "Transmutation"***
***Active: Ddiogelu (protection ward), Elfenol Streic (elemental strike), Tarian (defense boost), Hurtio (stun)***

I LIKED that my screen had adapted to the way I thought of myself more of a mage than as a witch, and that, while still not super impressive, my stats were moving along nicely. Soon, I would need to make time to check my scanned spell book pages and see if there were any new spells I could learn at this level.

"So…?" I turned to Steph, waiting for an answer regarding the blowjob—that she hadn't finished, I wasn't about to forget.

"That might have been more me than the curse," Steph admitted.

"Any time you two want to stop batting eyelashes," Ebrill cut in, gliding to land between us and the statue of Kordelia, "we have work to do."

Was there a hint of jealousy in her eyes? I nodded, mind reeling with confusion over the female situation here, but very glad to have any sort of distraction from the fight going on.

“Right, just…” I searched for something cool to say, but she gestured to the statue and growled as a burst of blue light shot out from her hand, then ran through the nearest demon, seemingly sucking its life force from him and delivering it to her.

Without another moment’s delay, I knelt, hands on the roof. Searching deep within, I connected to it all and made the concrete and metal, everything I could, rise around us so that we were in a cocoon of materials to defend against the enemy’s attack.

For now, at least, it would hold.

# 17

As the barrage continued around us, my barrier all that kept us safe, I quickly filled Steph in on what had been going on with the sleep, and how we thought it was a clue to finding the Liahona.

"Which we're not entirely sure we should even be looking for," Ebrill pointed out. "But… it might be the only way to wake Kordelia."

Steph nodded, glanced at me and asked, "And you, what do you think?"

"Until yesterday, I thought I knew you, thought you were just a regular girl. Then, until a few minutes ago, I was convinced you were evil this whole time, just using me. What the hell do I know?"

"Still… what does your gut say?"

I looked to Ebrill, sighed, and said, "That there's a reason these dreams are happening. That whatever the reason was for the Liahona being gone, it's over, and we might need to wake Kordelia to find out why."

"Or the answers might come in your sleep travel," Ebrill said.

"Each time, with the sleep… it's not long enough."

"With all this," Steph motioned around, the sounds of attacks on the building as others tried to break in, "I don't see that changing."

"Unless… you two hold them off."

Ebrill frowned. "What?"

"You two work together, keep them off us long enough for me to get the answer we need. Can you do it?"

Steph and Ebrill shared a worried look but seemed to agree. Steph nodded and turned back to me. "We'll do our best."

"That'll have to do." I turned to Kordelia, confused but ready. "When I dream, what exactly do you think is happening?"

"You're opening up memories," Ebrill said, "but… being there. The strange part for me is that I have no idea if you were in those situations the first time or not, since I don't fully have the memories. So, you're either time traveling, or accessing my memories in a way that unlocks them, but altered."

"A form of time travel, perhaps," Steph added.

Ebrill seemed unsure but nodded. "It's possible, maybe, that his transmutation power is working to fix my memory in this odd way."

"Yes!" Steph leaned in, eyes showing her excitement. "And that's the key to finding it."

"The Liahona," I said, unease crawling up my spine. "Everyone seems to want it, even knowing it's so… dangerous. Can we be certain this is the real you, now?"

"You never really knew me, but going forward, I hope

that can change." Steph put a hand on my arm, earning a glare from Ebrill that she ignored. "But you saw a side of me that is the only side I hope to show going forward. We're on the same side, Jericho, and I want to kick their asses for doing what they did to me, and to you."

"Good enough, at least for now," I said, and chuckled. "Well, here goes. Try to keep us alive while I go under."

A barrage of attacks hit at that exact moment, causing the remaining *shisa* to tense up and growl while Ebrill's hand lit up blue, and Steph's red. With a wave of Steph's other hand, several death wraiths appeared and dashed out through the stone mixture I had created to guard us, the sounds of steel on flesh following a moment later. Explosions came, too. Our little fortress rocked but held.

"How many of those can you send?" Ebrill asked.

"Seven," Steph replied. "But I can replenish them… as long as I have energy."

"We'll have to keep up your energy, then." Ebrill stepped over, hand on the other woman's cheek, and smiled.

It was clearly an odd moment for Steph, but as blue energy flowed into her, she went with it, closing her eyes and forming more death wraiths as her others perished on the other side of the walls.

I was about to get to it, when a voice carried from the other side. "Are you a pearl, now, boy?" Fatiha, but… raspier. "Do I have to pry that clamshell open and pluck you out?"

"This won't go the way you hope," I replied.

She laughed. "Oh, silly Jericho. It already has, in every… single… way."

The frown of confusion on Steph's face matched my

own, and she stepped up to the wall. "Let me out of here, so I can tell her what I think of her plan."

"No," Ebrill countered. "You might be strong, but alone out there…. No. Right now, we need to focus on this—on getting Jericho back."

A barrage of attacks sounded, during which Steph closed her eyes again and sent wave after wave of death wraiths out. Even with Ebrill's power refueling her, it was only a matter of seconds before both dropped to their knees, spent. The *shisa* nudged Steph's side. A new round of energy flowed from it, and she grunted, pushed herself up, and waited.

The attacks had stopped. Silence carried on for longer than a moment.

"Ignore them," Ebrill said. "We need to get you back… asleep."

"Seriously?" I replied, considering how drained they were.

"Sweet dreams," Steph said, nodding for me to get to it.

I chuckled, but more at the thought that I had no idea how I would actually fall asleep amid all the chaos. My heart still thudding, I lowered myself to the roof, unable to take my eyes off Steph and Ebrill. These two beautiful, amazing women were going to fight off anything that came my way, right? They could handle themselves, as they had proven.

Yet, there was some serious power out there trying to get at us. The *shisa* could help but I still wasn't at ease. I was about to push myself back up to say we could try again later, that this wasn't going to work, when Ebrill lowered herself to my side, put a hand on my forehead, and whispered the same spell that Fatiha had cast on me earlier.

This time, though, as Ebrill said, "Gorffwys" and my surroundings faded to dreamland, I embraced it as a pleasant warmth tingled through me, a quick dream as my mind hazed and I imagined Ebrill's hands in many more places than just my forehead.

## 18

In the third instance of me going back in time, or to Ebrill's memory, I appeared in a bed. Ebrill was sleeping on her side. For the longest time, I lay there, watching her sleep, until her eyelids fluttered open and she saw me there.

Her mouth moved, her eyes showing confusion, but then, instead of saying anything, she leaned in and kissed me.

I blinked, caught off guard by that.

"They had me convinced that I was hallucinating," Ebrill whispered. "That you only existed in my imagination."

"I'm as real as you." My hand went to hers between us, feeling her smooth, gentle skin. Odd, how it felt so much more delicate, almost fragile, compared to her gargoyle self.

She brought my hand to her hip and allowed me to move it, to…

Someone cleared their throat. I turned to see the

redhead from before. At the moment, I couldn't recall her name.

"You're back."

"Wait, you saw me last time, too." I frowned. "How were you going to try and make Ebrill sound crazy?"

"You remember my name?" Ebrill asked, grinning wide.

"I do." I paused, smiling and holding her gaze.

"And I'm Aerona," the redhead said. "Sorry, but… there was simply no sign of you. We had to assume you were an illusion or something. Maybe a ghost."

"Yet, you tried to tell me it was in my head," Ebrill said, turning on her friend.

"Ebrill, you know you're fragile, you know—"

"Fragile?" I practically laughed at the word in relation to her. When both looked at me with frowns, it registered that I had done something wrong. "What?"

"She…" Aerona hesitated, looking over to Ebrill, then closed her mouth.

"I have a disease," Ebrill said. "They aren't sure what it is, exactly, but the doctor is certain I won't last long. Maybe a year, tops."

"Something tells me you'll live much longer," I countered with a chuckle.

Neither seemed to appreciate the humor, considering that they didn't know about her existence far in the future, but that triggered my memory and reminded me why I was there to begin with.

"The Liahona," I said, looking them straight in the eye. "We're going to need it."

Both immediately reacted to the word, although in different ways. Ebrill perked up, eyes going wide, while

Aerona pounced, took me by the shirt, and had a glowing wand in my face.

"You should not know such a word," she spat, eyes full of disdain. "Tell me why I shouldn't kill you."

Mind racing, the only thing I could come up with was the truth. "Ebrill sent me to get it, to wake Kordelia, and maybe others. Seven in total, including those two. From the future, I guess."

Aerona's fierce, blue eyes moved from side to side, scanning me for any sign of lies, but finally she lowered her wand, then concealed it in her robes where it had been hiding before. She spun on Ebrill. "Explain."

"How can I?" Ebrill asked. "He's speaking nonsense."

"You must have said something when you last met, cast a spell that skewed his memory, something."

Ebrill shook her head. "Although, this does explain, in a sense, why he continues to show up and fade as he does. Some sort of strange, magical travel."

I nodded. "And if you could tell me where I am…?"

The two ladies glared at me for a long moment, then Ebrill said, "Avalon, of course."

*Avalon* sounded familiar, but as hard as I racked my brain, it wasn't connecting. Maybe Avalon was some city in England? My magic was still doing the voice-translation thing, so I wasn't actually sure if they had accents, and couldn't figure out how to turn it off.

"Come, we'll show you," Aerona said. "If you're who you say you are, then you might be the final piece of this puzzle."

"Where to?" Ebrill asked.

"He needs to meet Rianne."

"Are you certain?"

Aerona glanced back my way, then motioned us on. "Only if he's telling the truth. At the moment, I'm taking the chance."

Ebrill allowed a hint of a smile at those words, so I did too. Even more so when she took my arm in hers and whispered, "Stay by my side. I'll keep you safe," and offered a wink.

I chuckled, nodded, and we walked on.

We exited what appeared to be a guard post, since others were stationed outside with more along the wall, which seemed fairly far out there. These guards were tall and lean, some with dark skin and shocks of white hair. When one passed without a helmet and eyed us, it took me a moment to realize that her ears were pointed.

"Drow?" I asked.

"The best guards that money can buy," Ebrill replied. "That seems to disturb you."

"It's just… where I'm from, they aren't on the same side as you."

"Oh?" Aerona shook her head. "Never have trusted them, but nobody listens. They haven't given us trouble for as long as anyone can remember, and are worth every ounce they're paid."

"But you don't trust them?"

"That's right."

"I don't understand," Ebrill cut in. "Why would they turn on us?"

"Sorry, I can't answer that. I'll just say to be careful. Keep an extra set of eyes on them."

With a nod, she continued and led me to a path where I froze, unable to believe what I saw. Not far out were walls with more guards and soldiers posted, but beyond that was a long stretch of moving shapes and fires scattered throughout in the dusk light.

"What am I looking at?" I asked.

"The invading armies," Ebrill answered. "We've been under siege for months now, but more armies arrive by the day."

It reminded me of the house back in D.C., but on a much grander scale. "Why are they invading?"

"To get the Liahona, to control Avalon and its magic."

"I thought we were in Avalon."

Ebrill grinned. "Exactly. And the Liahona is the key to its magic. If you watch closely, they'll attack soon."

"We shouldn't waste time," Aerona said.

"It's dusk, it won't be long." Ebrill pointed to a group that had started moving toward the wall. "There, see. Must be a new group."

As we watched, they began their assault, only to be surrounded by a thick fog of purple that swept down on them from the hills. Screams rose from below amid the clang of steel on steel, and Ebrill pulled me close.

"Are they… fighting themselves?" I asked.

She nodded. "The magic defends us, as long as we control Avalon. Which means, as long as they don't get their hands on the Liahona."

"I saw how the magic destroyed them. I don't see why we should be worried."

"We've been successful, for now," Ebrill said. "But they're bringing in everything they have, including some sorcerers of great power."

"Surely, nothing we can't handle," Aerona said, flustered.

She led us on again. Soon we were at a wall of wooden

posts that was sharpened at the top. It was much smaller than anything I would have expected from a place like this, but as we entered I got the impression we were not at the home of the magic but more of a forward operating base. The inside was made up of crude buildings, a larger one with a standard out front showing a tree surrounded by a spiraling golden light.

A woman stepped out from beneath this banner, power emanating from her hands as they motioned me forward. The power resonated outward, her orange and yellow robes flowing back from her like the sunset incarnate.

"Rianne," Ebrill said, voice almost a whisper. "This is her."

For a brief moment, my heart seemed to freeze as Rianne's eyes met mine. A flash of orange and yellow crossed her eyes and then was gone. She motioned us forward and we approached, others now appearing behind her who might have been there the moment she stepped out, or might have been there the whole time—I couldn't tell.

We stepped up to meet with Rianne. She stood tall but looked at me as if we were old friends.

"If we don't save the Liahona, all of civilization will come to an end," Rianne said, as if she had been able to hear our conversation. She turned to address her followers. "Or, that's the story we've all been told."

"What do you mean?" Ebrill asked, looking at her with wide eyes. "I was under the impression that this was our last stand. Where we would defend it to the end."

"There's more to this man you see before you," Rianne said, indicating me. "I've foreseen his coming, and he will be the one to usher our world into an age of light. An age where the enemy only exists in shadows, in stories people tell at night to scare their friends and children. You will take the Liahona, Jericho, and in so doing will banish their kind from our world… for now."

"I don't understand," I admitted.

"They'll find a way to return, but it will be far from now, at a time you are familiar with. At that time, you must be ready. We are weakened, too far gone already and, as you might know, we have traitors in our midst."

"There has to be a way we can fight," Aerona growled. "It can't end like this—"

"It won't," Rianne replied. "You will return to fight. Stronger, more powerful. But first, you must do as I say. I've seen every possible outcome. While I cannot guarantee success, I can guarantee that every other way ends in failure."

"What do we have to do?" Ebrill asked.

"Bring the Liahona to the edge of Avalon while I hold off the enemy. There, a spell will be cast to end the presence of darkness on this planet, by removing Avalon and the Liahona."

"Aside from you, only Gertrude knows how to cast such a spell," Aerona said.

"Gertrude?" I perked up at that, thinking no way could it be the same person. But when a flap to a back room opened and she stepped in, I had no doubt. "How…?"

She looked younger than the version of my aunt I had known, but not by much. "I'm sorry, do I know you?"

"This… this doesn't make sense." I turned to Ebrill for help, but she shook her head, lost.

Rianne, however, spoke up. "It will, in time. For now,

go with it. Gertrude will accompany you with the rest of the team acting as your guide. You all must reach the Heart of the Mountain, where it will all make sense. Reach that spot, and the enemy will not be able to touch you—although, you might find a new enemy."

"Meaning?"

"Legends… a legend of a protector under a curse."

My eyes went to Ebrill, as I knew from the future that she had a special way with curses. She, however, looked lost.

"But… you won't be coming?" Gertrude asked, taking Rianne's hands in her own. There was an intense intimacy there, one that made me see my aunt in a whole new light. Also, standing there with this woman from an ancient, magical time and place, made me realize that maybe referring to her as my aunt had been wrong all along. At that point, though, it had been so long—even if she wasn't my real aunt, I didn't care. Thinking of her in any other way felt wrong and confusing.

"I will defend our position here, keep them off your trail as long as possible," Rianne said, and kissed Gertrude on the forehead. "We may see each other again one day, but… under very odd circumstances." She looked around. "It's settled, then. Gather the others and prepare to make the push through the pass. You must reach the heart of the mountain by morning."

Aerona nodded in firm confirmation but Ebrill's eyes showed worry. This wasn't some simple escape the house mission, it was much more complicated. Whatever I had just become involved with was part of a battle between good and evil, and I was in the center of it.

# 19

Gertrude, as I had taken to thinking of the past version of my aunt, led us to an armory, where they geared up. Interestingly, it resembled the armor that the future gargoyle versions of Ebrill and Kordelia wore, although with more layers of clothing. Unfortunate for my eyes, but probably good for their health. The large woman, Yenifer, took up a spot at the door to keep watch while the men gathered weapons.

"Avalon," I said to myself, then met Ebrill's gaze as she fastened a sword belt around my waist. "Not the same as King Arthur and all that?"

She frowned. "Never heard of any King Arthur. The current ruler of nearby lands is Emrys Wledig, also known as Ambrosius Aurelianus."

The name didn't ring a bell, but I imagined that, with the link to magic and the Welsh connection, this had to be the same as the legend of Arthur. Maybe he hadn't come along yet, or maybe that was all bullshit.

"We don't answer to them, though," Aerona said,

apparently having overheard. "Too many problems of our own, as you might have noticed."

Nodding, I chuckled. "Indeed."

"Let's get you a robe, at least, so you don't look so out of place," Ebrill said, guiding me to the corner where several robes hung.

I picked out a brown one, very standard and not out of place. "It'll do."

"This is so exciting!" Ebrill said, eyes on mine, hand taking mine to hold it between hers. She didn't seem to care about the robe one bit. "I still can't believe you were real, I mean, those other times you showed up… all in preparation for this moment."

"I'm still not sure I believe it myself." Leaning in and lowering my voice, I added, "What if I told you in the future, you… I mean, you and I are fighting another war, like this?"

"I would say that sounds like exactly what's supposed to happen, right?" She laughed. "If they get to the Liahona now, we're all doomed. But you're going to take it from here, expel their forces, then rally us so we can fight anew."

"Right." I pursed my lips, not sure that any of this made me feel comfortable. While I had recently learned new magic spells, me being in charge of some incredibly powerful magical artifact and being the one to use it to fight off some evil army, or whatever would be left of them? "So, what Rianne was saying…" I froze, not sure if I should voice it out loud. Essentially, what we were about to attempt to pull off would mean the end of magic on Earth, at least as these people knew it. We would be ushering in the age of men, a time when nobody believed in magic.

Legends would be born, myths of a magical land where Arthur would go off to in his final days. Fairy tales, basically.

Would any of it exist? Based on the time I came from, the answer was yes, because I had been born with some form of magic. Then again, maybe my birth or something to do with when the Liahona was to return had ushered in some return of this magic? Could the Powers That Be have known this was coming, and as each day approached they grew stronger?

If so, this trip to the heart of the mountain was only the beginning of my journey. At least I would have this woman at my side, and in her gargoyle form no less.

She was staring at me with a quizzical look, but when she realized my mind was back with her, she smiled. "There you are. Is everything as it should be?"

I nodded. "Worried, is all."

"The road ahead will be dark, perilous…" She pulled me close and kissed me on the cheek. "And while I'm glad to have you here to protect me, I'm not exactly defenseless, I should let you know."

My grin was enough to make her move in for another kiss. This time, her smooth lips pressed against mine. How odd that this version of herself had no idea that future her had given me a hand job already. It was like I had a secret from her, with herself, and that thought was a turn-on.

When movement came from below, I had to remind myself that this wasn't the time or place. We were about to make a push for some location that sounded dangerous, and in theory we could get seriously hurt along the way. For some reason, it never even crossed my mind that I might die until later. Maybe it was the distraction caused by such beauty around me.

And that only got worse. Or… better?

The door opened, and two more female elves entered. One, I instantly recognized as Kordelia. The other was a stranger. Behind them came several others, a mix of male and female.

I nodded at Kordelia, who noticed but pointedly ignored me. Odd.

"If everyone's ready," Rianne said, taking up a position in the center of the room, "let us begin."

Her eyes held a sorrow that didn't make sense, except that I knew what was coming and assumed she did, too. This land, if it was really Avalon, was about to vanish from the Earth. This much was confirmed as Rianne briefed the newcomers, indicating me as the one to take the Liahona from this world.

"Him?" Kordelia asked, skeptical. The other one, who I now could better see, wasn't bad to look at in the slightest. The warrior of the group, I guessed by her broad shoulders and the two axes hanging from her belt.

"You can't sense it, but his magic is strong," Rianne said.

"Does that explain the clothes?"

I was about to defend myself but Rianne laughed. "Oh, Kordelia, you'll understand much sooner than you realize."

That earned a confused look from the latter. Considering her tough demeanor even next to the warrior lady, it was a kind of fun look on her.

"There's no simply waking up from this." Rianne faced me, eyes heavy with sorrow. "This is the only way, I know that. But promise me you will find us, that you will do what is right."

"I promise."

With that, she placed a hand on her chest. Blue light appeared there, glowing brighter as it formed a sphere until it was as large as a balled fist. She took the light, held it as the glow faded to what looked like a ball of metal, and then held it out to me.

"I offer you the Liahona, so that it might guide you to us when the time is right."

I took it, nodding, feeling the light metal in my hands. "What now?"

Rianne turned to her fellow ladies. "We get you to the mountain's heart, where we will wait to defend the key to Avalon. The land will call upon us when it is needed most."

"Yenifer," Rianne said, giving her a pleasant nod. "It's an honor to have you fighting for us, as always."

"Thank you, high priestess," the large woman with the axes replied.

"We'll find Irla on the way," Aerona said. "She was out on a scouting mission."

"You will need her," Rianne said.

Aerona nodded in understanding.

"If that's all, then, you should be off. The time is at hand."

As if on cue, a gust of wind blew through the cracks of the structure. There was no doubt that wind spelled danger. As the ladies and the two other men in the room had already gone to the door, throwing it open and charging outside, I followed. Before exiting, though, I turned to the familiar sound of chanting.

There was Rianne, arms spread and robes fluttering against her body as wind pushed around her, purple and blue magic flowing like streams of light as it lifted her off the ground.

"Out, now!" Ebrill shouted as she grabbed me and pulled me with her.

As soon as we exited, the place exploded outward. Rianne rose into the sky, and the wood, along with her streaming light, shot out to target what I now saw were flying beasts moving in for the attack.

Whatever power had been keeping the enemy armies at bay was now gone—the Liahona, I realized. If I failed, all of the sacrifice that was about to happen would be for nothing.

# 20

Armies charged after us in pursuit, ranging from goblins and dwarves to monsters that rose from the ground in bursts of lava and darkness. Drow that had so recently been our allies suddenly turned on us, and winged beasts like I had encountered on the rooftop of my aunt's place swept down from the skies.

No matter what they threw at her, though, Rianne held off wave after wave of the enemy, her magic lashing about in bursts like solar flares, then swirling around that camp, luring more of the enemy to their deaths.

"Stick together," Aerona shouted to our party. "If we move as one, they can't stop us."

I glanced back, wondering how she could say that, considering the sheer weight of numbers against us. Had this been only a couple of days before, I would have been curling up and screaming, maybe rocking back and forth and thinking it was part of an episode. Now I had magic, though, and knew I was a bit of a badass.

*Let them come,* I thought, casting defense as I prepared. At least I would figure out a way to take down as much of their army as I could before falling.

Two rock trolls came rolling down from the hillside to our left, charging us to do battle, as a line of flying beasts caught up to us and made to block our route. Yenifer had both axes out and leaped to catch one on the back of a flying beast, using that as leverage to swing herself onto the back of another and start hacking away. Aerona and Gertrude sent explosive spells at the rock trolls, while the two men with us took up the rear with me and Ebrill, as goblins and orcs riding on deformed creatures that reminded me of hogs and panthers caught up.

I slammed one of these weird mounts with a stun spell that sent its rider tumbling right into the path of one of Yenifer's axes. Turning to attack another, I ducked as blades flew overhead only to vanish and appear swirling around a man's head as he descended on us. He thrust out with a hand and the blades attacked again. One of the men on our side pulled me out of the way as a shield of flames burst out to burn his attacker, but he took a slice across the other arm in the process. One of the other riders connected with Yenifer and knocked one of her axes to the ground before receiving a blast from Aerona that removed his head. I was somewhere between shock and determination to live, casting stuns in every direction I could think of. In that moment, I swore to myself that I would learn some legit attack spells as soon as possible.

Yenifer recovered her axe and knocked her attacker to the ground, but was distracted by another attacker, this one riding a wild boar. The man on the ground shifted and pointed his hand at her, and I knew something bad was coming if nobody intervened. Everyone seemed busy, and I was too far away.

Still, I took a step toward her, shouting. My foot hit a loose stone and I had an idea. After quickly stowing the Liahona within my new attire, I picked up the stone, used my elemental strike spell to fill it with fire and threw it, all in one fluid motion.

It hit and exploded like a grenade. Maybe too much power, I realized, and also understood that I wasn't as helpless as I'd thought.

The force sent Yenifer off balance, so that Gertrude had to step in to stabilize her. Combined, that duo was a force to be reckoned with, casting spells left and right while Ebrill and the others led the charge forward.

I paused long enough to pick up as many pebbles as I could, then filled them with the fire spell and threw them as we charged. Lines of those beast riders met my mini-grenades, and now we were advancing with speed.

"Nice work," Gertrude said, giving me a nod of approval before sending two counter-spells at an enemy who had just sent a wave of fire our way. The wave broke, replaced with a horse of ice that dove at the spell caster. He brushed it aside, but it was all the distraction Aerona needed to land a burst of wind that sent him into the air, flying far enough away that he wouldn't be a bother to us in the near future, if he even survived the fall.

I dove for cover as two Drow joined the dagger-magic guy, and threw myself behind a rock outcropping alongside Ebrill.

"On three," Ebrill said, nudging a larger rock my way

with her foot. Clanging of blades on rock sounded, and then we were up, her doing a defensive spell while I imbued the rock and sent it flying. The three attackers were blown away, at least two arms separating from bodies, a haze left in their wake.

"We have to keep moving!" Ebrill shouted.

"She's right," Gertrude added, charging past us from where she left four corpses in her wake. "Form ranks! Push on!"

Her hands thrust forward and created a beam of light around us that then shot forward as we charged again, so that the light was like an arrow that knocked our enemies out of our path. Aerona had a spell like a wake of fire trailing out to give pursuers pause, but our enemy had their own spells and were pushing on.

All the while, my heart was about to explode, my eyes bugging at the insanity of it all. Back on my aunt's roof, it had been night and maybe part of me hadn't quite accepted it. Here, though, we were in the midst of the magic battle, surrounded by massive displays of magic and armies of creatures that I had thought could only exist in fairy tales.

Ebrill met my gaze and shouted, "Too much for you?"

"I have a few tricks up my sleeve," I replied, and hit a flying beast with a stun spell, sending it to crash into the rocks behind us.

"You can do better than that," she said with a laugh, then caught a rock troll with a blue blast that made it solidify into one giant stone.

I nodded, scanning my screen for what spells I had learned, glad that the screen wasn't visible to others. How anyone ever memorized all of these and kept track of them, I couldn't begin to understand. Just then, I noticed another level up! That meant even more potential spells at my disposal. I quickly added the points and assessed my spell screen.

The screen showed that my level could access a specific set of spells, and I realized I must have either scanned a certain portion of the book, or it was adapting to meet my situation. This seemed the case because the new spells I saw were now related to stone and ice magic. Higher level spells included Frost Footing and Ice Wall.

The new screen showed the old spells, but I skimmed over those, reading:

***Level 4 MAGE***

***Statistics***
***Strength: 13***
***Defense: 10***
***Speed: 10***
***Luck: 8***
***Charisma: 8***

***Mana: 400***

***Recent Spells***
***Gorffwys (sleep); Frost Footing; Ice Wall***

I TURNED the corner and saw a line of Drow with arrows at the ready, releasing as one. As the arrows flew, they transformed into purple flames that penetrated the first wall Gertrude threw up but fizzled at a defensive spell from Ebrill. Another volley came from our left and I spun, managing to try the ice wall spell at the last minute. Arrows hit and exploded so that ice hit us, but nothing deadly.

Aerona led the counterattack with magic, Yenifer with weapons. The first group of traitorous Drow managed a counter-spell that sent her magic to burst into flames at the mountainside, but an attack from Ebrill and then Gertrude left their skin bubbling, some collapsing with hands clutching their throats. I tried my frost footing spell on the other group as Gertrude spun and threw a wall up to protect us, then I followed with another wall. When both faded, the result of my other spell was a hilarious show of Drow trying to regain their footing. Some were slipping, others had their feet seemingly frozen in place.

We moved while we had the advantage. Aerona and Gertrude attacked while Ebrill worked defensive magic on us, and I joined in. If she was doing so, that likely meant more trouble, soon.

Yennifer shouted as she charged, and I turned to see why. Three more rock trolls were being led our way by a horde of goblins and orcs, several of those flying beasts above them. She didn't wait for us. Boost spells from Ebrill hit her as she charged. By the time she connected with the first goblins, she was twice her size and glowing green, her axes trailing flames and ice.

I tried the sleeping spell on the rock trolls but with no luck. All it did was turn their attention toward me. My frost footing spell, however, was genius against the massive creatures and their heavy steps. The first time I cast it, one of them fell to take out a handful of the goblins leading it, and the second goblin caught the third and knocked it over with a swinging arm.

The two men in our group cut through the goblins and orcs with swinging attacks and quick movements that left them like a blur in the enemy ranks, and spells rained down on the enemy from the ladies behind me.

One of the rock trolls recovered and nearly caught me as it lumbered up from my right. A spell from Gertrude bounced off it. The strike tore through my ice wall and hit me in the chest, sending me flying back.

Luckily, my stats upgrades, defense boost—and maybe the fact that its attack had slowed thanks to my ice wall—kept me alive. Another strike came at me and this time I went deep within, reaching through the ground and connecting to the beast itself, for a moment taking over! Holy shit, I had just warged! It turned around and struck a flying creature like a baseball, sending it to slam into more of their allies. I wasn't strong enough to hold the rock troll, I realized as I was kicked out and back to my spot on the ground, feeling drained.

Ebrill was at my side, pulling me up, eyes wide. "How did you do that?"

"Magic," I said, moving my fingers like jazz hands in my semi-delirious state, feeling like I might pass out.

She laughed, pulling me with her and placing a glowing hand on my forehead. "Do it again, will you?"

A rush of energy flowed through me and this time I *was* the stone troll, turning on my companions and smashing the first across the jaw, then pummeling into the next and slamming it to the ground. Neither hesitated to fight back, but both had been caught off-guard by my attack and were at a disadvantage. One died after I got its head on the ground and gave it three good stomps. The other plowed into me and we rolled over goblins, squishing them as we grappled, and then he pulled both fists up, about to bring them down on my head.

"Get out!" a distant voice ordered, and I was back at Ebrill's side, watching from a distance as the rock troll obliterated the other's head.

My energy waned, but another touch from Ebrill and I was at least strong enough to walk.

"That was amazing," she said, and we watched as Aerona and Gertrude hit the remaining rock troll with enough explosive magic to end the last of them. "You're not hurt?"

I shook my head. "But you think I would've been if I'd stayed in there when it was killed?"

"It's beyond my area of expertise, but better not to find out the hard way."

"Agreed."

A glance around the mountains showed that we had done a fair amount of damage against our pursuers. While they regrouped and tried to break past the walls we had put up, we were able to make an escape. We fell back to another path through the hills, only to see a figure with streaming light forming, blocking out all but a silhouette. I was about to attack but Ebrill placed a hand on my shoulder, her eyes focused, waiting.

"Irla!" Ebrill shouted, and the light faded as their friend Irla appeared and ran over to embrace Ebrill, then turned back to the rest of us. Her eyes showed a mixture of confusion and determination.

Seeing the look of determination in my eyes as my hand moved to cover the bulge of the Liahona where I'd stowed it, she simply nodded, then turned and joined us as we charged down that path.

## 21

We entered a valley next, slowing as we went. The enemy wasn't in sight although the clouds overhead were swirling. My heart thudded. Irla and Aerona led, keeping watch, while Yenifer and Ebrill fanned out at my sides. The others were behind us. Our only injuries so far seemed to be on the soldier who had saved me, who I had since heard Gertrude refer to as Riland, and Aerona seemed to walk with a bit of a limp although it didn't slow her down.

"Don't let your guard down," Gertrude said, moving behind me with cautious steps. The shadows danced across her smooth skin, light catching her armor in occasional flashes. She wasn't the woman I knew from my time, that was for sure. I had to wonder what had changed between this time and then.

"I've cast a cloaking spell over us," Ebrill explained. "It'll take them some time to locate us but it won't keep them off our trail for long."

Working our way down the gravelly hillside, we passed an area where gnarled trees grew out of the hillside at an angle, likely from strong winds that were giving us a break at the moment. It reminded me of a beach we had visited on the way to my grandparents' house when I was younger. Skipping along, playing with my cousin Sarah, my dad singing "The Sky Boat Song." That had been a much simpler time. But, looking around at this team, at what I was part of, I wouldn't trade it for all the peace and simplicity in the world.

"Tell me your story," Riland said, walking closer now, his posture more relaxed now that he knew we were cloaked.

"Not much to it," I said. "Until very recently, I didn't even know that magic existed."

"One of them," Ebrill said with a chuckle.

"Excuse me?"

"No offense meant." She gestured out to the mountains far in the distance. "Past those peaks, there's a land of men who don't believe. But… I take it you're not from there, exactly."

"My land… Isn't discovered by our type, yet."

That earned a confused look from Riland, but he gave a grunt. "You learn fast. That's good. Stick close to this one," he gave Ebrill a nod, "and you'll be safe. Healing, defenses, you name it. Then there's Yenifer—one of the best warriors alive. I say one of the best, only because she and I haven't gone toe-to-toe yet."

Yenifer heard this and scoffed. "Riland, you get your sword anywhere near me, I'm yanking it off for a trophy."

"Not what I meant," the man said, but chuckled. He

gave me a wink, which I took to mean he wouldn't mind getting his 'sword' near her.

"And Rianne?" I asked.

"She can take care of herself," Ebrill replied, but glanced back the way we had come, unable to hide the worry in her eyes.

We reached the bottom of the valley and turned left, moving along where foliage above hid us from prying eyes.

"Rianne has been fighting the good fight since before many of us were born," Yenifer explained, eyes roaming the areas above for trouble. "The day she's gone from this world is the day I'll truly worry for my safety. Until then, not a concern."

"Is that why you fight so ferociously?" I asked. "Not worried about taking a killing blow?"

Yenifer chuckled. "I fight like I do because it's what I love. What I know. It's not the only thing I put my all into."

This time it was her turn to wink, and I couldn't help but notice the jealousy with which Riland eyed me after she had turned back. No time to dive into it, though, because we came to a ledge that led down to an area of red stones that bottomed out and then peaked again. Here, the clouds moved in, hovering just under the edge of the hills and giving the area an atmosphere of peaceful calm.

"The heart," Aerona said, sharing a look of excitement with Gertrude. "This is it."

"On me," Gertrude called out, leading the way.

With each step closer, the area in the center became

clearer, until we were close enough to see that there were rings in the stone around the heart.

Gertrude was the first to enter the ring, but immediately her feet sank into the stone. The two men rushed forward to pull her free, and now all three of them were sinking fast. I held my hands out to keep the rest back, not sure what to do.

"It's a curse!" Ebrill shouted, hands thrust out and glowing green as she apparently tried to counter it. "My power's not enough."

"They knew this would be our only move,"

"We did," a voice said from behind, and we spun to see Fatiha standing there. Not the Fatiha from my time, but one with tendrils of shadow magic streaming from her like a long dress as she floated above her army. It was the same woman, but somehow way more powerful. "None of you will ever leave this spot."

A mage at her side thrust out his staff and rings of red rose from the ground, hitting the two men and Gertrude. All three were consumed by the rocky ground, becoming one with it, merging until they were gone and in their place the rocks jutted out, sharp.

I shouted, enraged and confused. Gertrude was supposed to live, to be there when I showed up at the house. She was supposed to help me figure out how to use the Liahona, to save everyone.

Now she was gone and it was up to me.

"If I can just..." Ebrill charged forward, pushing against an invisible force, hands stopping the curse from taking her, and from letting the ground absorb us as it had the others. As it had my aunt.

"Maybe I can help," I said and accessed my

transmutation power, attempting to transform the curse, to use it to our advantage. Indeed, it transformed, but even as it did I realized the irony in the situation. Instead of killing us, the curse was transforming us. Or rather, them. I pulled out the Liahona, gusts of wind and debris flowing around me as the curse hit the others. Ebrill was still pushing forward but her fingers were growing claws, and horns emerged from her head.

A thought made my gut clench—I was the one who turned them into this!

But we were through, charging past the now-visible rings carved into the stone. We had made it past their barrier and overcome the mage's spell—at the cost that those remaining looked like demons with their horns and tails, and skin in purple and blue. One piece of the puzzle didn't make sense, though, or didn't until I heard the words Fatiha spoke next.

"You can't keep my magic from working," Fatiha shouted after me. "My magic is strong, and with the last of it my curse will see them changed to stone. Wait and see!"

How little did she know, while I was well aware of what would happen next. They would be stone, all right, until I managed to wake them far in the future. Even then, they would be stone each day, only flesh at night.

It was the price they paid to get me here, so I made the most of it.

"I'll find you," I shouted to Ebrill. To all of them, really. "Trust me. I'll find you and wake you."

The last of them turned back on the enemy, now in full gargoyle mode as they fought to keep me safe. Like the eye of a storm, the winds and debris continued to blow all around me, pushing even Fatiha and her army back. They dared not enter the nearby area, now that they had seen what happened to my team. Or was it something else? I took a step forward, moving for the center of what appeared to be a room carved out of stone with openings on one side and water visible far below.

Only, it wasn't so far below, I realized. It had been but was now rising fast.

Waves crashed up against the side of the mountain and sent water spraying past the caves and the openings. Some of it flowed in, so that my knees were wet as I knelt and began to chant. I wasn't sure what, exactly, as I touched upon my transfiguration power and let it flow. It felt like I was speaking in tongues as the words emerged and created a spell of their own accord.

In a flash, the water rose around me, the land folding, spinning, and expanding, and then a burst of magic shot out from the Liahona. A doorway opened and it all froze. Light hovered in the air and the water stopped mid-flow. Only I was moving. A glance around showed that the ladies, poised in their defensive positions and ready for anything, had completed their transformation to stone.

If not for my knowledge from my timeline where I had first met Ebrill and Kordelia in the exact poses I saw them in at that moment, this would have been even more shocking.

It wasn't only me moving, I realized. Somehow, Fatiha was pushing forward, moving through the magic of the curse. She was growing in form but in a way that made her seem like shadows and blurred light. My first instinct was to attempt stuns and other spells, but nothing worked. They all fizzled away as soon as the spells hit the magical wind. I tried using my transmutation magic as I had before, but all it did was vibrate through me in a way that let me know what sort of power I was dealing with here.

She was strong, and I was fucked.

Unless… My eyes went to the Liahona in my hands. It was opening this portal, supposedly doing something that would cause the magic of the world to change. If I could redirect some of its power at her, maybe… As I thought it, with my transmutation well already open for access, a blue beam shot out at Fatiha.

Her eyes went wide. The light and shadows faded, flowing through the light and back at me and into the Liahona, until she collapsed just outside the circle of my stone friends.

"No…" she muttered, and then slouched in defeat.

My power told me one thing about her at that moment —she was no longer a threat. I had stolen her magic, and now it was time for me to finish the mission. I went for the doorway that shone like an opening of light, floating there and calling me to it.

As I paused in front of it, the waves crashed again and this time rose, flowing all around me and the portal, surrounding us and carrying Fatiha and the others away. My magic told me that there had been a major shift. I closed my eyes to reach out and feel my surroundings. It was true—the armies of darkness were gone, mostly defeated. Others pulled back and retreated into the shadows and underground even as waves rode over the land, submerging much of it in magical water.

Avalon was no more, although it didn't seem to have ceased to exist. It was simply not there anymore, not where it had been. It was as if the water had taken all of

Avalon to another place. Maybe that would make sense to me in time, but for now, I only knew that I needed to keep my end of the promise.

I clutched the Liahona to my chest with both hands and stepped into the portal.

## 22

"It's not a vault," I said, waking to find the *shisa* eyeing me, Ebrill and Steph both standing over me. "It opens the way to Avalon. A magical land, where—"

"Where Rianne will be waiting," Ebrill said, eyes flooding with excitement as memories hit her.

"You remember?" I asked.

She nodded. "The rest of us… couldn't make it back. When Avalon vanished, only she stayed."

"And the attack here?" I asked, realizing that all was quiet. "What happened?"

"On pause," Steph said. "Although it might be the calm before the storm."

"Is that… it?" Ebrill stepped toward me, hand out, eyes on the Liahona.

"It is." First, I connected with the building and moved our protective layer aside to get a good view around. No attacks came. In fact, it was a peaceful night. The moon shone large above and the twinkling lights of a business not far off reminded me that some people were simply going about their lives while mine had been completely thrown on its head.

I took a step toward the statue of Kordelia, memories flashing of the real her, and how odd it had been that I hadn't known her at all when I went to sleep. So much had changed, while here it seemed that barely any time had passed. With a glance back at them, I held up the Liahona. "We're ready?"

Ebrill nodded, then Steph. The *shisa* nudged my leg, reminding me that it was there. I scratched it behind the ears, impressed with how soft its fur was, then pulled up my screen. In part it was to get this going, and also to move my focus away from how creepily large the *shisa's* red eyes were. My screen had the option to wake Kordelia, so I selected it.

Blue light glowed from the ball in my hands, then from her as the stone started to crack. Ebrill moved up next to me, hand on my shoulder, and the power flared. In an instant, Kordelia was free! She rose from the stone, roared as she stretched, and then turned to me, the blue light fading from her as she became a normal gargoyle.

Her eyes met mine, and she considered me. "Seems you were destined for greatness after all. What is this place?"

"The future," I replied. "And… in a sense, Gertrude's house. My aunt… I thought." Turning to Ebrill, I added, "But—"

"She died," Ebrill replied with a nod. "And yet, she was here…"

"My guess," Steph chimed in, earning her a confused look from Kordelia, "is that although she died in our timeline, it didn't affect the actual past where she once lived. Our timeline isn't affected by going back in time, in a strange way."

"So... not following the *Back to the Future*-style travel at all," I said. Now both Kordelia and Ebrill were looking at us like we were nuts. I shrugged, realizing there was no way we could explain all of that to them at the moment. "Point is, Gertrude was still alive in my time, until recently. I don't understand how that's possible if she died in my past."

"And you thought she was your aunt?" Kordelia asked.

I nodded.

"Too bad. She was always known to be good in the sack."

Ebrill hit her playfully. "Don't tell him stuff like that about his aunt."

"If she even was his real aunt. We all knew she had no sister, and... judging by this time period, wasn't from here."

As far as I could guess at it all, she was right. Gertrude had managed to escape the curse and set out to find the others. Maybe her memory wasn't all there either. Maybe it came back in bits and pieces as she found them. She hadn't been my real aunt at all, but found a way to insert herself into my mother's life—the estranged, well-off sister—after discovering a young boy was born with a magical connection that had the potential to turn this magical war around.

Or had she seen me in the past and been waiting all this time to find me when I was born, and then put the pieces in place to get us here? It was all a bit much to process, but I felt the puzzle coming together as though my transmutation magic formed the bonds, drawing lines and giving it light.

Kordelia turned to Ebrill and then Steph with a look of confusion. "I know one of you, and recognize this man." She glared at Steph, then demanded of Ebrill, "Who is this, and where are the others?"

"Others..." I repeated the word, not as a question. It hit me that the others had indeed turned to stone as the spell finished and I was taken out of the heart of the mountain, transported back to this spot. "You think we can find them?"

Her glance my way was even more confused.

"We don't know," Ebrill admitted, turning back to me, then Steph. "Did you hear anything while under their influence?"

"Bits of my time under the curse are still with me," Steph said. "But that side... no, they didn't have the answers. If anyone, that'll be—"

"Gertrude," I interjected.

"I still don't understand it," Kordelia admitted.

Realizing that there was no getting around at least attempting an explanation, I traced a line in the air, using my transmutation power to make an actual line of blue light appear. "Imagine it like this. Even with going back in time, we only affect our time going forward. Never truly the past. But that doesn't explain why I was able to fight, why I was able to take the Liahona."

"Unless that's how it always was." Ebrill looked about as confused as I felt.

"Or she didn't actually die back then," Steph offered. "In either timeline, I mean. In that case, you *did* take the Liahona, and maybe had it in the other timeline, I don't know. We're dealing with magic here, so... your movies and the so-called rules of time travel might not make the most sense."

I frowned. "We saw her, but..."

"Again, magic. Healing. Who knows. It's possible, though, isn't it?"

"Actually, we didn't see her corpse," Ebrill admitted. "Only her being absorbed by the stone."

Wiping away my floating timelines, I grunted. Maybe my time explanation wasn't right, but it was cool.

"What matters is that we know what we have to do," I pointed out. "We need to get my aunt back."

"So, she's not dead?" Kordelia asked.

"We think she is." I chuckled, realizing how ridiculous this sounded. "But in our timeline, the future where I met you all... she died. However, she left behind some sort of magical version of herself."

"Perfect. Where?"

"That's the not-so-perfect part. With... Fatiha."

"She's here?" Kordelia snarled, claws bared. "Can someone tell me what exactly is going on? What are we up against?"

I did my best to fill her in on what had happened so far, stressing the point that Steph had been under a curse and hadn't acted on her own when attacking us, and that Ebrill hadn't had her memory regarding Fatiha. About how my dreams had taken me back in time, to a world where Avalon had still been part of it, and apparently dark and very different types of people and creatures had roamed the Earth.

"We have the Liahona," Kordelia said, processing it all.

"Why can't we simply open the way, find Rianne. and restore access to Avalon?"

"Only one person knew how to do that," Ebrill replied.

"Gertrude." Kordelia considered this, then nodded. "We have to go after her, then."

"Exactly. And... how do we get her back?"

"And we don't know where to find her," I added.

Steph cleared her throat. "I might have an answer to that. And it... might relate to some of the rest of our problem."

"Meaning what?" I asked.

"They've found the heart. The heart of the mountain, I mean. They haven't been able to access it, but have certainly tried."

"Right...You mentioned that the enemy knew of at least five, but didn't know where. It would make sense that at least one or some remained at the heart of the mountain. Maybe the others were accessed later by some spell Gertrude put together, or maybe some were cast into our world by the initial magic that sent Avalon away. I don't know."

She nodded. "And whatever caused them all to become stone also put some sort of protective spell on it all."

"Whatever caused them..." I shuddered, looking first at Ebrill, then Kordelia. "It was me."

"What?" Ebrill asked.

"Me. I caused it. Or, rather it was the Liahona and the only way I could keep it safe."

Ebrill looked at me with confusion that slowly became a look of fascination. Kordelia had a hint of a smile, the type like one has after figuring out the answer to a riddle.

"Shouldn't you be mad at me?" I asked.

"No," Kordelia said. "Because it was the only way. If that's how it happened, Rianne knew it was the way."

Ebrill nodded. "She put all of this in motion, after all."

Steph, too, was staring at me in a new light. "Break the spell and get them, or get them and break the spell—I'm not sure which comes first."

"But breaking the spell might give the enemy access to the heart." I frowned. "Do we know what that does? What it means?"

"Access to vast stores of magic," Ebrill replied. "We've talked about it."

"But, like this?"

She nodded.

"If you can make it there and free her, there's one more for your side." Steph glanced at Ebrill and then Kordelia, scrunching her nose as if trying to decide whether that was a good thing or not. "The enemy, as I knew them at least… we can access their hideout."

"If we can access it and find the one behind this," Ebrill's eyes lit up with excitement, "we get access to Gertrude, and then restore Avalon."

"And find the others," Kordelia said. "Find Aerona, for one. She's powerful, and we could use her on our side."

"We could use them all on our side."

Kordelia nodded. "No one's denying the effectiveness of the rest."

"We open the door, we find the others?" I asked.

"I'd actually bet that most are in there," Kordelia replied. "We can speculate all day long, though, and it wouldn't do any good. Best get on with it and go from there. So, if this girl says she can get us where we need to be, I say we listen."

"Morning will be here soon, though," Ebrill countered. "If we're going to attack, we all need to attack."

"She's right," Steph agreed. "We'll need everyone to stand a chance."

"It's agreed, then." I was actually relieved to not have to go on the offensive until the next night. "But… why aren't they attacking right now?"

"I'm not complaining," Steph said with a chuckle. "I'm famished."

"Actually, I could eat," I admitted, and had to take a wicked piss. After, I connected with the *shisa*, sending a request that the guardian keep watch on the house. The rest of us cautiously made our way to the kitchen. I paused from time to time to sense whether there was an attack or any of the enemy nearby, but we seemed to be clear.

Soon we'd each had chances to use the bathroom and our bellies weren't empty. Ebrill looked at me thoughtfully and said, "Is it possible…?"

"What?"

"I'm just thinking out loud here. Maybe something to do with your last dream, or travel, caused them to pull back from the attack?"

"Like my helping back then caused their power to diminish now, too?" I licked some truffle mustard from my lower lip, still relishing the taste of the turkey sandwich I'd made for myself.

"It's… maybe possible," Steph said, but held her hand up and made a line of fire appear from her palm, tracing it around her fingers. "Although, it doesn't seem to have affected me."

"No need for assumptions," Kordelia said, and then

pushed her half-eaten sandwich away. Apparently, she wasn't as into my 'cooking' as I was. The other two had devoured theirs. "We need to be sure of what happened. Go back and see..."

All eyes went to me.

"I'm not sure I can go back," I admitted. "Or if it would be smart. It was getting pretty crazy in there."

"We know," Ebrill said. "We were turned to stone."

"But we need to know what the enemy is up to," Kordelia chimed in. "And this might be the best way."

"Or be pointless." I turned to Steph, hoping she would take my side on it, but she pursed her lips, looking to the window.

"Night will be over soon," Steph pointed out. "We might want to take the opportunity while we have these two here to help guard, and to break you from your sleep, if needed."

"Shit." I held up the Liahona, frowning. "We're sure we even want to open it?"

The stares from Ebrill and Kordelia were answer enough. I sighed, nodded, and followed them back to the bedroom.

"I just woke up," I pointed out.

"That shouldn't be a problem." Ebrill stepped up to my side, lowered me to the bed and then whispered, "Gorffwys."

Only, nothing happened.

"Huh," Steph said, scratching her arm. "Maybe he's growing strong against it?"

"Might be my transmutation," I admitted. "Haven't exactly learned to master it, and before I knew it was magic, this kind of thing would happen. More with sickness and stuff, but I could see how a sleep spell might be something my subconscious pushes back against."

"Well, shit." Steph eyed Kordelia, who shrugged and leaned against the wall, hands on her temples.

Ebrill joined her old friend. The two spoke in lowered voices.

As they did so, Steph approached, eyeing me mischievously and licking her lips. "Not all of it was me, but… I remember a certain way that helped you sleep."

"Yeah?" I asked, not catching on at first. When she sat next to me, pushed me back, and undid my belt, it all came back to me.

"Maybe this will help." Steph licked her lips again, then reached down and pulled out my cock. Her hand stroked it, her eyes focused as if this were our first time and she was studying it, hoping to never forget it.

"It is, you know," she said. "Our first time, more or less."

"Are you reading my thoughts?" I asked.

She chuckled, eyes moving to mine as she continued her caress. "No, just guessing what you're thinking. For me, having been under a curse before, this is kind of my first time."

"You don't remember any of that part of it?" Ebrill asked.

Steph blushed, as if having forgotten they were with us. Her hand went lower, caressing my balls as she leaned against me, head on my chest. "Somehow, there are… bits and pieces. Almost like I remember the sensation, the emotions, but like I was reading about them. I want," she looked up at me again, "to experience it all."

"And them?" I asked, eyes going to Ebrill, who eyed me, then Steph, waiting.

"You're… with her, now?" Steph asked.

"I don't… know. Ebrill?"

"As much as we want to be," Ebrill answered. "And that doesn't have to be exclusive."

"Oh?" Steph eyed me, then Ebrill, and nodded. "Me neither, I guess."

"Yeah?" Ebrill looked over at Kordelia, who was eyeing me uncertainly.

"I'm not ready for this," Kordelia said, standing up and going to the door.

"Kor," Ebrill said, going after her.

"Have fun," Kordelia said, turning and holding up her hands. "I don't want to get in the way of that, but… I just woke up to find the world completely changed. I can't —not yet."

She left, but Ebrill turned back to us. At first the look in her eyes was distant, but when they found me again, it was hungry.

*Not yet.* Those words stuck with me, my cock throbbing at the thought that she would one day join us. That was saying something, because I was already rock-hard from Steph's touch and the sight of Ebrill still in the room.

The gargoyle bit her lip and took a step closer. She undid her armor, exposing her lavender breasts with their purple nipples. Another step, and she paused, watching Steph kneel before me, take my cock and run her tongue around the tip. I closed my eyes for a moment, relishing the pleasure, and when I opened them again, Ebrill was nude, bare below, and kneeling at Steph's side.

"Allow me," Ebrill said, kissing my hip and then moving in to the base so that both had their tongues running along my cock, eyes on each other.

Steph pushed my cock to Ebrill, watching as the latter took it fully in her mouth. My eyes flitted back and forth between Ebrill working my cock and Steph undressing, removing her top first to let her petite breasts free, then shimmying out of her skirt and pulling off her boots.

"You don't have to," I said, pushing myself up, unable to believe this was happening. After seeing the darker side of her, I never thought I'd see her beautiful nude body again, let alone have the chance to touch it. To kiss her breasts and grab her ass as she rode me.

She smiled wide and straddled me, angling her hips to run her wet pussy along my cock. "When you've been through what I have, watching a cursed version of yourself… well, you know… it's like watching someone else eat the perfect slice of tuxedo cake. Try and stop me."

My laugh turned into a moan as she slid her pussy down around my cock and started working her hips. Her perfect, petite body wasn't new to me, but it was a sight that would never fail to fully arouse me. Small breasts shaking with each thrust, dark nipples that almost didn't seem to fit the paleness of her skin, and more ass than someone her size deserved. That ass slapped against my thighs as she leaned back, letting my cock hit her spot, and then she rolled over so that I was riding her as Ebrill watched.

I closed my eyes, getting into it and trying not to think about the fact that I was being watched. Suddenly, there were lips on mine and hands running through my hair, along my chest, down around to my ass. Ebrill was there, joining in, while Steph lost herself in the bliss and threw her head back, moaning, shaking, and then laughing. There wasn't even a moment's hesitation as she scooted out and pushed me toward Ebrill, and my ex—no longer my ex?—propped herself up on her side, watching us and gently caressing herself as Ebrill and I started to caress each other.

My hands found Ebrill's voluptuous breasts and then I sucked on them. She lifted me with her insane strength, so that I almost felt a bit out of place as she threw me to the bed and leaped onto me. It was wild, and as she flipped us over and pulled me on top of her and thrust my cock into her pussy, I got into her rough ways. I enjoyed it as she then flipped us over again and started riding me with more ferocity than I had ever experienced in bed.

Seeing as she hadn't been laid in many, many years, I supposed it made sense. Steph started moaning again and I saw she was fingering her clit while watching, and damn, that turned me on. I took control then, turning so that both Ebrill and I were sitting. I grabbed her ass with one hand, breast with the other, and loved the sensation of her warm, wet pussy gliding up and down on my cock.

A creaking sounded from the doorway, and I noticed a figure standing there, the door mostly shut, as if she didn't want us to know she was watching. I threw Ebrill back, imagining Kordelia there, caressing herself as she watched my shaft sliding in and out, my balls bouncing. The fact that a soft moan came from that direction a moment later made me even more into it, and before I could move into another position, I buried my face into Ebrill's breasts, hearing moans from all sides, and then pulled out just in time so that my cum shot over the gargoyle's stomach.

She laughed, rubbing it in, and then licked one of her fingers with the cum on it. “Delicious.”

I chuckled nervously, hands still running up and down her thighs as I stared into her eyes. When I looked toward the doorway, Kordelia was gone.

Steph kissed my neck in response, watching as Ebrill reached to caress me.

“I’m glad the sleep spell didn’t work,” I admitted as I reclined, spent.

Ebrill laughed, hand stroking me even though I was pumped dry. “No, I don’t think so.”

“No, definitely… not.” Finally, cock throbbing and smile spread across my face, I fell back, asleep with a protective hand on the Liahona in my pile of clothes beside me on the bed.

* * *

THE DREAM TRAVEL wasn’t like the other times. Pulling, twisting… light swirling. Pain ripped at my soul, unlike anything I had ever felt, and then I was free of it, but floating in darkness that cleared in places as a heavy fog would to give brief glimpses of one’s surroundings.

“You don’t belong here,” a female voice said, and for a moment there was another form moving with me in the darkness.

The darkness gave me a glimpse of what I knew was the heart of the mountain, submerged in the water that surrounded the land that was Avalon. The forces of darkness were confined to sections of magical mist. The others moved about in confusion. Their world had been torn apart, pushed aside from its normal place to another plane of existence, a world of magic separate from our world, where magic no longer had a place.

And I had played a part in it!

"That's exactly right," the voice said, returning to my side, circling me and laughing. "You, Jericho, brought down the walls of this world. Is that backwards?"

"Who the fuck are you?" I spat out, not in the mood for these games. "We did what was needed. We won."

"Ah, but at what cost?"

While I didn't want to admit it, this figure had a point. I hated to see this land of magic cast off as it was, and everything I was beginning to understand that it represented. And as she materialized further, her words rang even more true. Maybe that was the hypnotism of her beauty, this striking woman with her green eyes, red hair that flowed about her as if in a bath, and glimpses of nude flesh amid shifting darkness.

"Who are you?" I said, my voice almost slurring.

"I go by many names, none of which you need to bother yourself with. But come to my side, join me… and I'll tell you one. A name you'll enjoy, a name you can call out as I make you shout with pleasure."

She came closer, body almost in full view, hand out to touch my face. But I pulled back, shifting and turning away from her.

"They will lead you astray," her voice said, distant now, fading. "Mark my words. You want me at your side. You *need* my power."

"All I have, all I need… I'll figure it out without you."

A jolt shot through me and I was pulled back from that place, leaving it all behind.

* * *

EBRILL WAS THERE, watching me. Steph was up against the wall with her arms around herself, while Kordelia stared out the window.

"It was bad," Ebrill said, holding a cloth to wipe my forehead.

"I sensed her," Steph added, a shiver running through her body. "The woman with the flowing red hair."

"You've..." I pushed myself up, still shook from the pain and confusion of the dream. "You've met her? Before?"

Steph shook her head. "Only her power."

It made sense to me, then. The curse—I would have been under its influence, had I given in. More power, maybe, but no freedom.

Kordelia turned back to me, then nodded. "It's almost sunrise."

Ebrill eyed the window and helped me up. "No more attacks, at least for now."

"Fatiha might come during the day," I pointed out.

"She might, but it wouldn't do much good." Steph shrugged. "Wouldn't be able to do much against us. Her side's power relies on darkness and shadows. She'll come at night, I'd wager."

"There you go." Kordelia went to the window, flared her wings, and said, "Be sure to get some rest, but be ready in case she tries something. You never know."

"Understood," I replied, and offered a smile to Ebrill, then felt Steph wrap an arm around my waist. She nuzzled me as the other two froze. We watched the sunrise, Ebrill and Kordelia now stone nearby. Out of curiosity, I reached out to mentally check on the *shisa*. The creature was still there, patrolling the grounds. I had been curious how that worked, but apparently the guardian didn't work like the gargoyles. That made sense, I supposed, since it was brought to life with my powers and the powers of the house, not some gargoyle curse.

My eyes moved to the way the orange light highlighted the curves of the gargoyles' statues. The shadows made me wish they were alive so I could caress them again, hold them to me. I reminded myself that they would be back at night, but that seemed so far away. Funny how this time, they had each struck a pose before the morning light transformed them so that they had a fierce, sexual look of danger to them. I couldn't help but let my eyes roam over their curves, now stone, before turning back to see Steph watching me. She raised an eyebrow.

"You and this one..." She walked over to Ebrill, running a finger along the stone of the gargoyle's arm. "It's serious?"

I laughed. "We barely know each other. But... it's complicated."

"Like how we're complicated?"

"We are, aren't we?"

She turned back to me, hand resting on Ebrill's shoulder, the other moving along her wing, seductively. "I was trying to find myself, back then. Looking for ways to expand my magic. I wish I could say it was to bring my mother back from the dead or something, but she's alive and well with my dad in the Peugeot Sound. For me, it was as simple as wanting power in the form of magic. I joined secret societies, a coven... all of that to find out I needed more. A journey to a land you never want to see earned me those wraith knights, and the fire was the result of a month in Turkmenistan. But this… everything I heard from anyone who knew anything about the Liahona pointed to more power than anyone could possibly comprehend."

"We've all done things," I said, not sure if I should be consoling her or what, but trying anyway.

"Before this," Steph turned, eyes focused on mine. "I crossed lines, maybe, but always for the right reasons. Or, so I told myself. When I got the power I sought, I told myself I'd stand up for the little people, use my new power to, I don't know, cure cancer or something."

"Thought you said it wasn't for anything like that."

"Not directly, but… yeah, in part. Can you really imagine having that power and not doing some good with it?"

"Of course, I would do good," I replied. "But then again, I'm not doing this for power."

"Keep telling yourself that." She scoffed, arms crossed. "There was a time, right when the curse hit me, and I was still more in control, when I would have hurt people."

"And now?"

"No more crossing lines. It's wrong, of course, but more than that—I set myself up to be susceptible."

"To their curse?"

She nodded. "Never again, Jericho. Never."

I took her in my arms. "You're with us now."

"I wanted power, and I got it." She scoffed, pushing me away, but accepted my embrace when I wouldn't let her. "At a price."

With a laugh, I gestured around. "Hey, we talked about

how it would be if you could come out here to D.C. with me. Here we are, living the dream."

She allowed a smile, but then her eyes flashed red and she looked at the door. "They took that from me. Now… I want to see them fall more than ever before."

"Let's do it, then." I held her hand and guided her out of the room. "We've let them lead the attack long enough. Now it's our turn."

# 23

During the day, while the enemy was weak and our gargoyles were asleep, Steph and I set out to locate the hideout. Only the *shisa* would be at the house to guard it, but I hoped my power would allow a connection so that I would be notified if there was trouble. I rented a car and drove out to Virginia with Steph, although traffic in the Belt was a bitch. At the moment, we were driving among tall houses with pillars, chandeliers, and all that fancy stuff I'd never been exposed to when growing up.

"You remember it being around here, right?" I asked, hating the humidity of the D.C. summer.

She nodded. "It's like there's a voice calling me back. A voice in here," she held a hand to her chest, "and it's… cold."

"The voice?" I thought about it. "That checks out."

Her hand reached out and found mine, although her eyes were focused on our surroundings. If she couldn't locate the enemy's headquarters, this journey would have been for nothing, but we had to try.

"I have to ask," I said as we came to a stoplight, waiting. No cars there, but that's how it goes sometimes.

"What?"

"The dunes..."

She laughed and bit her lip.

"So, you remember that?" I frowned, confused. "But..."

"Like the other times, not clearly. Not like it was me. When you say, 'the dunes,' I get these images like I watched a porn about two people going at it in a sandy, horrible situation." She laughed. "Hey, I'm not sad to not remember all of that—sand shouldn't be involved in certain activities."

"Those were your exact words when we were done!"

"Really?" She motioned for me to go, as the light was green. "I'm thinking... it's like it was still me, kinda like a zombie, you know? Basic instincts were still with me."

"You got me that snow globe from the lodge where we met..."

"Listen, Jericho..." She ran a hand through her long, now-white hair. "None of this is easy for me, but yeah, that's something I would've done. It's also something a fake version of me would've done, or cursed version, to try and earn your favor, right? So, I don't know what to say, because I don't know if it was a latent version of me making some of those choices, or someone else for me."

"Sure." I glanced over as we came to a fork in the road. Her eyes flashed red, and she indicated the road to our right.

"Going forward though, that's all going to be different. In part, because I'm sharing you with Ebrill, apparently."

"That..."

"That."

"So, it does bother you. Right?"

"Honestly," she gestured for another turn, "no."

"Why not?"

She laughed. "You want me to be jealous, don't you? Well, sorry. I'm the type of girl to get myself cursed in a search for more magic, to have a wraith knight army, in a sense. To be honest, Ebrill's hot. I kind of like the idea."

"Damn. Nice?" I laughed. "This is all uncharted territory for me. I don't know what I'm supposed to think."

"Shut the fuck up, then. You get two hotties licking your nuts, you cum and smile. No doubting or wondering what to think about it."

"True." I was all grins, until a thought hit me. "Wait, you and the wraith knights aren't...?"

"God, no." She hit me. "They're basically ghosts, if even that. More like forces with no other purpose but to attack —as far as I know, they were never actually alive. They certainly weren't my lovers, or aren't, or anything like that if that's what you were implying."

"Asking, not implying. And good."

She gestured for another turn. The houses were much larger and spread out here. She perked up, eyes searching, glowing a slight red.

"We're close?" I asked.

She nodded.

"Oh, shit," she said.

"What?" I turned, looking for what she had spotted, and had to swerve when I nearly went right into oncoming traffic.

“Nothing like that,” she said, then turned to me, frowning. “I just remembered… Beaverton. That night at your friend’s place.”

I stiffened. Both my body, and below. Instant wood as I recalled that drunken evening. We had gone for my buddy’s birthday and crashed in his guest room, and for some reason that was the night she had let me stick it in her ass. The next day she had been sore as hell, although neither of us had even remembered it until the day after that. She had been mad at me for a week, and I felt like a jerk for letting it happen while we were both so toasted. Then again, I’d been just as drunk and out of it, so I had a hard time accepting the guilt.

Still, now that I realized she had been cursed, the whole situation took on a new meaning. “Fuck.”

“Yeah, I’d say.”

“I mean, it’s hitting me that all of this—I mean, it’s horrible. In a sense, if you were cursed—isn’t that like I was fooling around with a drugged-up chick?”

“First, you had no way of knowing,” she replied. “Second… you can make it up to me.”

“Oh?”

“You’re hot, and you seem nice. Everything I remember from our time was great, but I seem to remember myself being more giving than you were. At my insistence, I know, but…”

“You’re hinting that you want me to go down on you?” I glanced over, then laughed when she didn’t respond. “Steph, you never wanted me to. I would fucking love it. Come on. You drive and I’ll do it right here, right now.”

She hit me again. “Shut up, we’re almost there. But

next time we're fooling around, it'll be the grand buffet for you."

A snort-laugh escaped, and we both laughed, then. I had to adjust my cock so my boner wouldn't be so obvious. She reached over, though, massaging it for a second before saying, "Shit, we're here."

I pursed my lips in a pout and pulled over to what looked like a large church. "No way."

She shook her head. "Not the church, but I remember passing it. One of these houses, for sure."

The heat and humidity hit me hard when we stepped out of the car, but not as hard as the sight of Fatiha in the park nearby. She sat on a bench, posture straight, staring at us with hands folded in her lap. Both hands, as she had somehow found a way to heal it back on, or grow another. Then again, this was all magic largely beyond my comprehension, so what did I know?

She was waiting.

"What brings you two so far from home?" Her voice carried, barely more than a whisper, but audible from far away.

We approached, reaching the gate of the park, where we stopped. "You can still pull back," I said. "Call it quits Nobody has to be hurt."

She laughed. "If your aunt had known how simple you were, I doubt she ever would have entrusted so much of her plan to you. Lucky me."

I glared, holding her gaze. After a few beats of this, I grunted. "Then we're done. One thing, though—how is it that my aunt didn't recognize you for who you are?"

"She only ever knew me as the one with magic," she replied. "When my magic was gone, or mostly gone, so was my imprint, the way she would have recognized me after so much time."

I scrunched my nose, processing this, then nodded. "And you… what, want your magic back?"

"So much more than that," Fatiha replied with an evil smile. "My powers, yours. All."

"For what ends?" Steph asked.

"Magic should never be hidden. Never be stolen, certainly." Her eyes penetrated my soul, boiling deep within.

"And never, ever be used to hurt others," I countered. "Unless they need to be stopped, unless they are the ones using it to commit evil."

Her lip twitched. She turned, waving me off. "You have until midnight to hand over the Liahona. We will come to collect."

We stood there for a while, watching her walk off. Cars passed, all oblivious to the fact that evil incarnate was hiding out so close to their homes. A breeze rustled the leaves above, as if none of the chaos mattered, as if peace could really exist in this world.

Of course, the Virginia heat and humidity served as an annoying reminder of what was to come. My hand went to the inner pocket of my jacket where I had stored the Liahona. With our powers, safer to keep it close.

"We're still coming for her, right?" Steph asked, opening the gate and going in to sit on a bench. I followed and did the same.

"You have a good idea where she'll be?"

Steph grinned. "One of my wraith knights is following her right now. If she still had her full magic, she would know—but she doesn't."

"Sly dog." I chuckled. "But, I thought your type of magic doesn't work in the day?"

"It works, but on a very reduced level. They could attack us right now and still prove to be a challenge, but with your transmutation spells, I can't imagine they would have much chance of success."

"Speaking of which." I pulled up my screen and focused on making transmutation spell options appear. "I'm hoping I can get more specific with that side of my magic. And..." Sure enough, a new page appeared. I gave Steph a satisfied nod.

"What do you see?"

"A few options, such as ones I already know. At my level—er, power level, I guess—there's what I've done so far, like animating objects as I did with the house, kind of."

"Badass, I might add."

"Ooh, here's a fun one. It looks like I can change the air to basically be poison, or even make it... solid?"

"So, you can attack people by changing the air they breathe, nice." She leaned back in thought. "I guess the latter can be used for shields?"

"Or making a temporary prison."

"Nice." She eyed me, waiting for more.

"Aside from that, it's mostly silly stuff, but... no way." I stared at the words for a moment, then grinned. "Shape-shifting."

"As in... you can actually become a wolf and stuff like that?"

I shrugged, glanced around, and tried it. My whole body was instantly wracked with pain, my skin feeling like it was being torn off. Blood formed in lines on my arms, and I stopped, staring in horror at what I had done.

"Fuck me," she said, eyes wide.

My mouth was dry, everything hurt, and I felt like an idiot. So much so, that all I could do was sit there and stare as the blood started to trail my skin, forming lines between hairs.

"What… was that?" Steph asked.

"A spell I'm never trying again," I replied. "No way in fucking hell."

She nodded, slowly. "Maybe when you're much more powerful? When you can heal? Speaking of… can you? Please, because this… is disgusting."

I almost laughed, but it was the sort of hysterical laugh that was almost a whimper. My screen was still up, and while I didn't see anything about healing on there, I focused on my wounds and timidly pressed with my mind. Nothing. Licking my lips and thinking instead of it like an 'undo,' I tried again. This time, while the pain was still lingering and blood still on my skin, the wounds closed.

"Undo," I said, and shrugged. "As close to healing as I can get, for now anyway."

With a sigh, she said, "I'm glad I don't have your magic. No offense, but… it's too much."

"I'm right there with you, at the moment."

A shimmer of light appeared, and movement as if a shadow leaped up, and then Steph shuddered.

"Your wraith knight?" I asked.

She nodded. "We have their location."

"Good." The pain was starting to subside, at least, so I stood and motioned back to the car. "Let's prepare for tonight. You should drive now, though. I'm a bit… shook up."

"I'd imagine." She caught the keys, moved to the driver's side and got in.

Once we were on the road, the AC blasting, I closed my eyes and relaxed, only noticing as sleep took me that the pain was finally gone. And this time, when I slept, there was no travel. Not even any dreams.

Just sleep.

# 24

We arrived back at the house before sunset and had a quick snack, then checked the place, and gave the *shisa* an appreciative pat on the head. The guardian seemed to enjoy that, then kept on patrolling. I connected with him for a moment, sending my appreciation and feeling that several observers had been detected while we were gone, but nothing more.

When my attention returned to my surroundings, I noticed Steph giving me a sideways glance. I was about to ask what that was about, when she ran her tongue along her lips and motioned toward the bedroom.

"A shower before the fight sounds good, don't you think?" Steph said.

I nodded in eager anticipation. We made straight for the shower, undressing as we went. She had it turned on and was cleaning herself before I managed to remove my pants. I only paused long enough to check on the Liahona in my jacket. In a moment, I was back with her, kissing her neck and then her breasts as one hand moved between her legs. She put one leg up on the side of the bathtub so I could move to my knees. My kisses moved along her thigh, then to taste her pussy. It was wet from the shower but also naturally, I imagined. My nose nuzzled her pubes. My tongue lapped her up, moving around her opening and then finding her clit as my fingers ran along her ass. She angled her hips forward, giving me better access, and then I fingered her while eating her out, loving every second of it. Water cascaded down her body and over my face, making it hard to breathe. I kept going anyway, kissing and licking and moving my tongue around until she pulled my hair, pushed my head into her and let out a high-pitched squeal.

"Now I…" She let my head free, so that I could take a big breath.

"Yeah?"

"Now I…" she managed between heavy breaths. "Now… I… owe you."

I laughed. "You'll get to it, I'm sure." A glance back out through the open door showed orange and purple streaks in the sky. "We don't have much time."

She nodded, but as I stood, she still managed to bend and give my cock a nice lick, then kiss. "When it's time, I'm going to suck you dry."

"I look forward to it," I admitted, soaping up as she stepped out of the tub to find a towel. Soon, I was out, too, drying myself off and trying to ignore my raging boner and the way she kept glancing over at it.

"Sure you don't want me to…?" she asked.

My eyes went to the window, the dark sky, and I let

out a sigh. Of course, I wanted to, but even as I thought it, the blue glow returned to the gargoyles and their stone broke free. Ebrill and Kordelia turned to see us, both naked but covering ourselves somewhat with towels.

"Really?" Kordelia scoffed. "Nothing better to do while we're out than fuck?"

"Actually," Steph countered, "we found the hideout."

"And didn't exactly fuck," I added.

Steph grinned.

"Spare me the details." Kordelia tossed me a shirt from my open suitcase. "And get dressed before you blind us all with your pale ass."

"I like that ass," Ebrill noted, finding the whole situation quite humorous.

Ignoring the comment, Kordelia strode to the window and looked out into the early night. "They'll be here soon, I imagine."

"Then we need to get on with our attack," Steph said.

"Actually." I held up a hand for attention. "I've been thinking. If we wait a bit, I can see about controlling the house from somewhere nearby, make it seem like we're within and putting up a fight. Then, when they're working to counter our barrier spells and break their way in, we're on our way to their base."

"And you think Fatiha will have your aunt at their headquarters?" Ebrill asked.

"She has to realize I know by now, and that I'll be after the tree."

"Tree?" Kordelia asked.

"It's... a long story. Basically, what's left of my aunt—er, Gertrude, is in some sort of magical tree. It's small. Fatiha wants the Liahona so she's pressing the attack, but if we get access to that tree and Gertrude, we open the gateway and gain access to the magic of Avalon. Of course, she'll press the attack, but also guard that tree with a strong force."

"Let's be ready for her, then," Ebrill said. "And be ready to make our getaway."

We all agreed, finished dressing, and made our way out of there. Steph had demonstrated foresight by parking the car a couple of blocks away earlier, and now we slipped out the new back—set up since I had rearranged the place with my transmutation magic—and kept low. Ebrill used her cloaking spell now that the memory of it had come back to her. At this point, she explained as we went, she felt that most, if not all, of her memories had returned.

We reached the perfect spot, hidden among the trees of a nearby house on a hill. From here, we could see my aunt's house and the surrounding area. At the moment, all was calm. Not even a wind to sway the trees, or a dog's bark to break the quiet. The purr of an electric car sounded. The car appeared down the street a moment later and drove by, but other than that, nothing.

As we waited, I glanced up to see Kordelia watching me. Curiosity mixed with maybe a bit of seductive interest. I nodded her way, and she cocked her head, eyes not leaving mine.

"What?" I asked.

"For a small man, you're… hot," she whispered. "And pleasant to look at."

"He's not so small," Ebrill said from my left, earning a grin from Kordelia.

"Not where it counts," Kordelia agreed, causing me to blush.

"I thought size wasn't supposed to matter," I interjected.

Steph cleared her throat, holding up a finger. "To an extent."

"Says the tiny woman." Kordelia licked her teeth, then shrugged. "Maybe to some it doesn't. To me, it does."

"Me too," Ebrill said. "I hate to be shallow, but… yeah. Good thing we're not working with a shrimp here." She cupped my package.

I frowned. "Aren't we supposed to be working, here?"

"They're giving you a compliment," Steph said. "Take it and say thank you."

"Thanks," I said but shook my head. "Now focus."

"Until they get here, does it matter?" Kordelia asked. "You focus on what you want to focus on, let me focus on you."

This time I turned in confusion. "Sorry, but… what? You left the room back there."

"Wondering if I made a mistake."

"Oh." I glanced at Ebrill, trying to judge whether Kordelia was fucking with me, but she was smiling my way like she was ready for more.

"There will be more opportunities," I said.

"Wait a second." Ebrill moved close to me and crouched at my side, hand on my abs. "Isn't it true that your powers kind of amplify when you're in contact? Like we did before."

I gulped and eyed her and then Kordelia, nervously. "Yes."

"Then it's settled. Kordelia, you can touch it."

"Hey," I started to protest, but Ebrill was already undoing my pants.

"It's not like we have to fight, here, or run. Not at first, right? You're going to connect to the building, make them believe we're inside, and make them regret sending their forces. So, this," she had my cock out—semi-flaccid, but clearly growing, "this will only help."

Kordelia looked to Steph first, who, smiling, gave her a nod to go ahead. Kordelia reached out. One cold finger found my tip, moved along the smooth skin, then traced it back toward the base as the rest of her fingers joined the first to wrap around it.

By that point, I was fully grown and had my hand on a nearby tree trunk for balance. My eyes closed as she gave me a gentle stroke, and then I was there, spreading out from the house and nearby streets, able to sense the incoming danger.

"They're here," I said, and felt her stroke me again. "Oh, my... Ohhh." This time the flash came with a line of surging darkness that pushed through the ground, forcing its way up as it moved for the house. I mumbled something about not stopping, and then felt another hand, this one on my balls, then a mouth, although I didn't know whose it was.

"Not so much that I break focus," I had to say, but hated those words at the moment. I wanted what they were giving me, but if we fucked up our attack, literally, everything could be ruined.

"Sorry," Steph's muffled voice said. The mouth then moved off my cock.

I was the house. I was old pieces of armor and blades, and moved through the floor and walls, even the outer grounds to rise and meet the enemy in their charge. They hit, then, and I unleashed. A bit too much, maybe, but then again, with three women's hands on me, how could I contain myself?

The first wave was completely immobilized, and I was pulled back to the gargoyles and Steph as I waited for another strike.

"What happened?" Steph said, hand under my shirt and caressing my chest.

Looking at her there, the other two with their hands on my crotch, I had to smile. "Wiped out the first round. No contest."

"Damn," Kordelia said, stroking me faster and harder now.

"Whoa, slow, slow," I said, feeling the tingles of an orgasm threatening to take hold. "Save it for the big game."

She laughed, going back to the gentle caress. "Suit yourself."

"Can you use your ice and other magic when in there?" Steph asked. "From the house, I guess?"

"I'll try." My hand up, I turned back to meet another incoming attack. "Here goes."

This time I was in there and ready for them with what felt like a haunted fun house. The floor undulated and the walls shook and smashed. I tried my ice magic but nothing happened, so I turned to my ability to warg. At first, I tried it on a demon, but was pushed back with a painful sensation. The way I figured it, the more intelligent the enemy was, the less likely I would be able to take it over. Or, maybe it had to do with magical power? Either way, I went instead for a lumbering brute of an orc and managed to make it work.

Three good slashes with its serrated sword ended three enemy lives, and then I was out as a blast of magic came its way. The orc exploded, but I moved through the walls, wanting to try something else. Seeing the caster of the magic, I tried warging again—it worked! My theory had been that magic users were drained right after using magic, so maybe that would be a time I could take over. In the body of this seemingly low-level sorcerer, I spun and let loose on the nearby enemies with my ice magic. I didn't have much, yet, but my frost footing hit and then I created several ice walls to block the enemy in, so that as they slipped about they accidentally cut into each other. Some even got mad and burst into a killing frenzy, so that I turned their less-intelligent fighters against each other.

"Where are you?" a voice said. It echoed through the house and then hit the body I was in, sending pain shooting through me until I was forced to pull out.

I was still one with the house, but couldn't tell where the voice was coming from. Instead of waiting to find out, I gave them one more round of haunted funhouse-style of attacks and pulled out. The first thing I saw when my vision returned to normal was that I had leveled up. We needed everything we could get, so I assigned points and checked to see my new spells. The screen read:

***Level 5 MAGE***

***Statistics***
***Strength: 15***

***Defense: 14***
***Speed: 13***
***Luck: 10***
***Charisma: 10***

***Mana: 450***

***<u>Recent Spells</u>***
***Gorffwys (sleep); Frost Footing; Ice Wall; Ice Claw; Frost Bite***

AS EXCITED as I was to find out how ice claw and frost bite worked, we needed to get our plan into action before it fell apart.

"Go!" I hissed, pulling my cock from their hands and putting it away with much regret. Kordelia let out a heavy sigh, while Ebrill gave me a mock pout.

"Don't die," I said as we started to move, "and we'll have plenty of time for that."

The idea that two women—gargoyle women, no less—were sad over not being able to play with my dick almost made me laugh. It was so unlike any reality I had ever faced. Then there was Steph, making it three, and we had our own weird background.

But what I said held some truth. We needed to live, or none of that would matter. We needed to succeed, or there would be worse problems.

# 25

The Liahona was wrapped up and tucked safely in my jacket's inner pocket, and the pocket zipped. We couldn't leave it behind, because we might need it if we found my aunt and needed to activate it at the last minute.

One hand on the wheel as I steered, I had my screen up trying to make sure I had my new spells down. My hand would try the motion of a claw as I said, "Crafanc" and then I would make a biting motion with my fingers as I said, "Brathu." Neither was loud enough to make the spells work, but I needed to be ready to cast ice claw and frost bite when the moment came.

Even when I took a break from practicing the spells, driving with the *shisa* in the middle and two gargoyles in the backseat of the car made it hard to see. When I swerved for the third time, Steph started to get annoyed.

"Focus on what's ahead, not behind!" she growled.

"I'm sure there's some sexual joke in there that needs to be said," I replied with a glance in the rearview mirror, then over at her. As we closed in on our location, tension was high and nobody was smiling. "Come on, this is the moment! We're making it happen!"

"Honey, babe," Steph squeezed my leg supportively, "I love that you're so into killing evil witches, but you're a bit over the top."

I laughed, but then noticed in the rearview mirror the way Ebrill was eyeing me. "What?"

"Just... the non-magics called us witches in our time."

"That bothered you?"

She shook her head. "What bothered me was the fact that there was no differentiation between the good and the evil. Clearly, the evil knew the difference—enough so that they had to attack us. Enough so that we had to all but eradicate them."

A *thump* sounded and the car lurched. The *shisa* growled, alerting me mentally to problems around us.

"All *but,* with but being the key word there," I pointed out. "They clearly made a comeback."

No argument from her there. Instead, she leaned forward and wrapped her arms around me from behind, head on the side of the seat. "When I first met you, I knew you were special."

"Did the clothes give it away?" Kordelia asked with a playful scoff.

"Maybe. But I mean that I knew he had a large role to play in all of this. I had no idea that he would awaken us in the future and open the gate to Avalon after it was exiled, but... a large role, certainly."

Steph glanced over, eyes going to Ebrill's arms around me. As much as she said it didn't bother her, I had to wonder. Or thought I did, but then she shifted and laid a hand on Ebrill's arm while staring into her eyes. I had to stay focused on the road as another *thud* hit the car and then a dark form appeared in front of us, causing me to swerve. We were being pursued, but still had a lead on the enemy.

"Together, right?" Steph said to Ebrill, and I couldn't help glancing over as her hand moved along the gargoyle's arm. Ebrill didn't pull back.

There was something intimate about that touch, and I couldn't wait to get this fight over with so I could see where it would lead. For now, though, I needed to know what we were up against.

"Fatiha has someone working closely with her," I said. "A number two. A strong mage, maybe."

"How do you know?" Kordelia asked.

"I took her magic, when I was back there. The Liahona took it, I should say." I swerved as a shadow appeared next to the window and suddenly slammed into it, causing the glass to crack. "Shit!" I swerved again as Ebrill lowered her window and cast a protective spell over the car.

"But she has… some magic, right?" Steph asked.

"I think she's getting some of it back, or maybe whatever she's using is not actually her, but this second in command? I'm not sure, but there's definitely someone else involved. My guess is we'll have to take him or her out."

"And I'd add that this other is likely protecting the tree from the home base." Kordelia clicked her tongue, adjusting to try and get a better fit in the awkward position she had to sit in.

"Meaning, we have our work cut out for us." I clutched the wheel, leaning in to see that the sky was now full of those shadowy forms, darting about above us and trying to hit the car, but held off by an invisible barrier.

"What happens when it's time to get out of the car?" Steph asked.

"Run," Ebrill replied.

"Will that work?"

"We're about to find out," I chimed in, seeing the church from before, then the park. "We're here."

"Stay close," Ebrill said, leaning back, arms off me now. "The protection spells are strongest the closer we are together."

"And remember, we need to make this fast," Kordelia added. "If we get stuck out here until sunrise, we're fucked."

"We make it out of here before that, we can be fucked, too," Steph added. "But in a good way, right?"

In spite of her wink and the way they all nervously laughed, I was too distracted for the joke—or flirtation, if she was serious—to affect me at the moment. My focus was on the street outside, where shadows were taking the form of witches and demons.

"They're coming in fast. We need to go now."

"Agreed," Ebrill muttered, then threw open the door and waved her hands as she shouted, "Ddiogelu!"

Protective barriers rose before us. We were out, then, the other two and the *shisa* running around the car to push forward toward the enemy line. I had my new spells at the ready, excited to have the chance to try them out. With the practiced motion and saying "Crafanc" as I thrust my hand, I sent out an ice claw. It formed blue light around my hand and then shot out, growing larger as it went until it was a hand of ice with long claws, tearing through the enemy and shattering behind them. Two witches fell, and the assault began. Other witches were casting spells that Ebrill was barely keeping off our backs, while Steph had her wraith knights on the attack and Kordelia was casting blasts of magic at the enemy. The *shisa* was growling with excitement, taking off in a blur to strike at the closest demon.

"Gotta love that dog!" Steph said as she stopped at my side and summoned wraith knights to tear into the enemy around the *shisa*. Not that it needed help, as already it was tearing into its second demon.

"Not really a dog," I corrected, but was more focused on casting an ice claw to hit successive lines of the enemy, and then spinning to shout "Brathu" and hit others with frost bite. Gales of wind and frost burst forth to rip through our opponents.

If not for the fact that my magic was more ice-based, I'd say I was fucking on fire.

My team was doing their part, too. The *shisa* ripped through the enemy forces like a streak of light, pausing after each group of four. Most weren't dead, but were left with one or both legs torn open. Some fell and received a second bite, their throats torn out. Kordelia and Ebrill were forces of magic and muscle, at one moment casting their spells as I had witnessed in the past, then using claws to rip their enemies to shreds. Each plowed through enemy fighters, knocking those aside that they didn't take the time to destroy.

Steph ran past me, shooting fire and summoning back two of the wraith knights who had fallen. She paused long enough to say, "Badass fucking team you've chosen for yourself!"

"They kind of chose me," I muttered, hitting a hellhound with the ice shot and watching as the fire went out and the beast shriveled up.

Screams registered, along with shouts from civilians, and it was only then that I realized they had likely been happening for some time. People were at their windows, pointing, and one house was already in flames. Sirens sounded in the distance.

I didn't know if this would show up as some insane supernatural event in the news, or maybe there was a magic way to make it appear like a natural disaster, but I knew we needed to get out of there.

As I turned to say so, a tree cracked, the ground thudded, and in charged a man three times as large as me with skin that looked to be mostly covered in stone. He wielded two chains with scythes on the ends, swinging them at us and not caring if he hit those on his side if they got in the way. Some of his people turned on him, but he was focused, barreling in toward Ebrill and Kordelia.

"Gorlon," Ebrill growled and then waved at us, pointing at the giant. "Hit him with everything you've got! Forget the rest!"

I complied, and as soon as I focused on the giant, the *shisa* homed in as well. Steph sent her wraith knights and bursts of flames, while I attempted the ice claw and shots. When nothing seemed to do any damage, my full arsenal went at him, at the same time that Kordelia and Ebrill went on the offensive. They took turns, leaping onto trees and houses and using ledges and branches as jump-off points to try and hit the giant higher, gliding on their wings in short bursts. Nothing we did left much of an impact, though, and when the giant saw that it couldn't hit the quick-moving gargoyles, it came after me.

Having a giant charge at me with swinging scythes wasn't exactly my idea of a good time, even with my amazing team doing their best to take him down. The rest of the enemies had pulled back, giving us room to see how this went down, only shooting the occasional spells when the opportunity arose. Luckily, with Ebrill's defensive spells and my ice wall, none made it through.

The giant reached me in several large, lumbering steps, and I tried frost footing. His next step slid, but he caught the ground with one scythe, nearly catching me with the next. When his eyes rose to meet mine, I almost regretted causing him an inconvenience—those large, gray eyes sparkled with tiny specks of black throughout. Again, he swung. I threw myself back and cast an ice wall, then tried changing the ground to pull him in. He was too strong, breaking through the wall and then pulling free from the ground.

Swords clanged out as wraith knights struck his legs and back, but he simply roared and took out three of them with one wild blow. More leaped forward, using each other for leverage so that two made it high enough to try attacks at his chest and throat, but a spell from a bystander took out one. The other landed with a sword in the giant's chest, but only a shallow strike that pissed off his adversary more than anything.

Steph was nearby. She summoned again, only to collapse to her knees as the newly-summoned knights faded. She was using her magic too fast.

"Ebrill!" I shouted, pointing to Steph while attempting another go of frost footing and then ice claw and shot, aiming for different parts of his body in hopes of finding a weakness.

A growl caught my attention. The *shisa* was there, having taken a break from trying to attack. Or so I thought. It shook its head, growled again, and then charged. An image of the earth moving to lift the *shisa* and throw it at the giant entered my mind, so I obliged. All around me, the earth was distorted like after a massive earthquake, and now it was even more so as I sent a wave through the ground that caught the *shisa* and tossed it up and at our enemy.

The giant slipped, the *shisa* hit, and then I saw that Ebrill had helped Steph so that both were up and charging. Kordelia glided overhead, and they all hit at once. I roared as I charged too, focusing on the nature of my ice shot and ice claw attack and working with my transmutation magic to forge them together and put them into the shape of a sword in my hands.

It was cold, but almost like part of me. The giant struggled to get at the *shisa*—even dropped one of its scythes—and then we all made contact, tearing and striking. My sword penetrated. As the ice of my blade sank into the stone, blue spread across the giant's body. The stone cracked from his skin and fell free.

He was exposed!

The attacks drew blood. Another lunging attack nearly caught me. That huge scythe slammed into the ground inches from my foot. I cast an ice claw directly at his face and watched as the icy magic tore into his eyes and forehead. His screams drowned out the incoming sirens.

The giant was down. The rest of the enemy was converging on us. But in other news, I had leveled up again! I quickly applied my stats and checked out my new situation, which read:

***<u>Level 6 MAGE</u>***

***<u>Statistics</u>***
***Strength: 20***
***Defense: 15***
***Speed: 16***
***Luck: 13***
***Charisma: 12***

***Mana: 520***

***<u>Recent Spells</u>***
***Gorffwys (sleep); Frost Footing; Ice Wall; Ice Claw; Frost Bite; Frost Shot***

"THEY'LL JUST KEEP COMING!" Kordelia shouted as I dismissed the screen. "Ebrill, you have to cloak us!"

"Give me room," Ebrill replied.

Kordelia was at my side a moment later, her hulking frame reminding me how intimidating she could be, especially with this fierce snarl of hers. She pointed to the incoming group of enemies, and said, "Walls, attacks, everything you've got."

I nodded and looked at Steph, who heard and shouted, "I'll recall my knights, and send them all at once to hold the wall as long as they can."

"Ready," I said. We all got into position, the *shisa* suddenly back at my side as if sensing what was to come.

"NOW!" Kordelia conjured a spell that sent debris—dirt and grass and stones—flying, creating a circle around us that would blind some, hurt others, but mostly set the barrier of where my ice walls needed to go up. I could do better than that, though, and made the ground rise first with my transmutation, then created ice walls atop the circle. Only flying enemies would be able to make it over, but they had to be damn powerful if they were going to make it through Kordelia's spell.

The wraith knights were already moving out, translucent as they went through the walls. Ebrill had a glowing hand in the sky, muttering her spell.

"We're covered," she said as the blue burst out forming a haze over us, and then we turned, Steph taking the lead.

"Where to?" Ebrill asked Steph, but she was looking around as she ran, unsure.

"I'm getting something, but… I think they've found a way to counter my knight."

My humor at her wording seemed ill-timed, so I attempted something, working with the *shisa* to pick up the magical scent of where the wraith knight had gone.

The *shisa* gave me one look and then ran, so I followed. My team was close behind as I rounded the church to see the *shisa* digging at a spot between the church grounds and the next house over.

"I got this," I said, and the *shisa* moved out of the way, eyeing me with excitement. The little lion-dog was really starting to grow on me. "Thanks, Shisa," I added, deciding that worked for a name. Why the hell not?

"Tell me we're not about to unearth some massive

tomb where undead will rise and fight us," Kordelia said, eyeing the church.

Steph laughed but shook her head. "As far as I know, that's not part of it."

My focus, regardless of what awaited us, was on the transmutation magic that worked on opening a way for us before the enemy managed to get back on our trail.

Earth flowed aside like it was the sea before Moses. Sure enough, it opened into a tunnel beneath. We shared a look of excitement and then went in, charging through the tunnel with our path lit only by the glow of blue from Ebrill's hand and orange from Steph's. I took the time to close our entry point but already the sounds of monsters screaming for blood came from ahead and behind. They must have found their way in through other entrances.

The tunnel led to a whole series of underground networks, tunnels and rooms. We charged through, hitting a group of demons who had been on their way to find us. They fell in a matter of seconds. We moved on until Shisa finally stopped in a round, tall room, growled, and started circling, eyes looking up.

I followed his gaze and saw why. A form appeared as a silhouette against a ceiling that was half there, half not, but stabilized as the figure passed through it.

It was Fatiha, I saw as the light from our glow lit up her features.

"You think you're so clever," Fatiha said, drifting down toward us, dress fluttering about her, eyes glowing red. She landed and let her silver hair down so that it flowed around her shoulders. Despite her age, it wasn't hard to see why I had once found her attractive. Although, now she was purely evil in my eyes, and that dimmed the attraction level quite a bit. She landed and gestured around us. "But, what sort of idiot would enter the lair of one of the Nine Ladies?"

"The nine witches of Ystawingun," Ebrill said, eyeing her. "I should have known."

"Not me, but I serve those who remain loyal." Fatiha smiled, spread her arms, and looked like she was about to hiss, when instead, a stream of fire emerged and circled around her before vanishing. "There was a time when I could do so much more than that. A time before... you." She glared at me. "That magic will be mine again, once you are disposed of."

All of this was a bit much to process, along with the idea that there was someone in this place more powerful than her. And if so, that meant this other was likely guarding the tree and Gertrude. It only made sense, so I had to go out on a limb.

"We demand an audience."

"What?" Fatiha frowned, put off.

"An audience with the witch who this hideout belongs to."

"The Nine Ladies, we called them," Kordelia said. "Not the type to take audiences, at least."

"You know nothing of my mistresses," Fatiha spat out.

"Don't I?" Kordelia laughed. "Apparently, you don't know, do you? About Rianne, about where she came from?" Fatiha's frown made that clear, so Kordelia continued, "Surely you're familiar with the two who abandoned the rest."

"The traitors." Fatiha nodded, curious now.

"Morgen was the well-known one, although she went

back and forth, didn't she?" Kordelia eyed the older woman, waiting to see if she would catch on.

"Mizoa!" Fatiha said, eyes going wide. "But… how? Rianne, she was before, no?"

"Not Mizoa, exactly. Rianne wasn't one of the Nine Ladies but was Mizoa's mother. In fact, it was learning of the betrayal by the rest of the Nine against her mother that drove Mizoa to abandon the group."

"What's your point with all this, Kordelia?" Fatiha asked. "You, who have been known to wade in both sides of the pond yourself."

"Not anymore. And my point is simply this—your master, whoever it is… She *will* see us, one way or another."

"In her time and place." Fatiha's fire suddenly went out as a wind blew through the passages and up to flow over her. She bowed her head.

"That time is now," a voice said, one I was sure I recognized from earlier battles, or maybe it had been in my head before? Either way, it wasn't new.

The wind picked up and then a ring of fire came together, nearly burning all of us but for quick spells cast by Ebrill and me. The fire formed one entity in the middle —a tall woman in a black gown singed by flames, with black eyes and hair held by a net of embers that glowed but did not burn.

"You requested an audience," the fiery woman said. "Granted. Now surrender or turn to ash. Your choice."

# 26

None of us moved, unsure whether to attack or run. Even Fatiha was frozen in place.

"Thiten," Ebrill said, nodding. "I know you all too well. Or, of your legend, at any rate."

"Well, then, we are off to a good start. I only know you as a statue, so..." Thiten grinned, wickedly. "What will it be? I'm guessing ash."

"If you mean, do we refuse to surrender?" I stood tall, as best I could. "You bet your ass."

She frowned, cocked her head. "It's been long since the Powers That Be have allowed me to roam out of my dark holding, but language sure is strange these days."

"This isn't possible," Steph said, fists clenched in a way that made small sparks trace her knuckles.

"What's that?"

"She..." Steph turned to Thiten. "You can't be here. I've read all about you, studied the same spells, and turned away when I read how they had contained you."

"Clearly, I am free," Thiten replied, and then sighed. "Enough toying with you. Ash it will be."

Without another moment's hesitation, the woman surged toward me, once again becoming the flames that had forged her. I thrust out with my newest ice spells, only to watch them shatter on the wall behind her as flames threatened to burn my skin. My saving grace was the ice wall I cast at the last second. It almost melted instantly but gave me enough protection that I wasn't completely fucked. When the next attack nearly hit Ebrill, I cast more ice walls, and Kordelia deflected flames with her wings as she worked to get in close. A good hit, almost, but instead of making contact she ended up on the other side, slammed into the wall.

"Obliterate them!" Fatiha shouted from where she stood watching.

"Gorffwys," I muttered, indicating her in hopes of the spell putting her to sleep. I shouldn't have let her distract me, though. In the moment it took me to cast that and her shield spell to throw it off, I was under siege by a string of fire spells. Each one grew in power over the last. I dodged, threw ice walls before me, and gladly took Ebrill's hand so that she could pull me out of the path of the last one.

Then I was on the attack, trying every spell I could. My ice sword nearly caught this ancient lady in the throat, once, but a flame shield rose and she vanished, only to reappear behind me. My transmutation took hold, letting me move through part of a wall to dodge her counterattack, and then exit at another spot farther along.

I was moving fast, maybe because of my enhanced stats from leveling up, or maybe because my life depended on it. Either way, I was starting to get the idea that this was too much for even us.

We all struck at once, and were all pushed back.

"Did you really think there was any winning here?" Thiten asked, rising above us with her fiery black robes flickering about. "Against one of the Nine? You?"

She pulled her hands back and it was like all the air had been sucked from our side of the room. Flames curled along the walls, building and starting to form waves of fire that came right at us.

"We tried," Kordelia said, determination in her eyes in spite of the defeated sound in her voice.

Steph growled and threw out another wave of wraith knights… only to see them fall as she, too, collapsed. I caught her, holding her tight as if that would protect her from the flames. Ebrill did the same to me, muttering spells.

Another growl, and then Shisa charged past. The lion-dog leaped for Thiten, and a strange thing happened—Thiten seemed to be met by a force field, sent flying back. I could breathe again, and the flames were gone.

Our enemy recovered but stared at Shisa with a mixture of curiosity and horror.

"I have an idea," Ebrill said, and knelt next to Shisa, hand on its head. The flash of light showed me she had given it an amplification spell.

Shisa froze, amped up by Ebrill's touch, and growled. An instant wall of blue light formed between us and Thiten, then surrounded her like a dome. She charged the wall, hitting it to be flung back against the far side, where she skidded to a stop. She pushed herself back up, cast fire at it, only to see the fire fade.

"No! You can't!" Thiten screamed, pushing at but unable to break through the invisible barrier created by Shisa.

"How...?" I started.

"As I said, this can't be the real Thiten," Steph pointed out. "But a summoning, a part of her brought here via a spell, that could be held off by the protective magic of a *shisa*."

"You have no right to talk about what I am or am not capable of," Thiten, if that was really her, said. "I will destroy you. Before this is over, I will hunt each of you down and see you torn apart piece by piece."

"Shut her the fuck up," Steph said, then turned back to me and the other two. "It's not her."

"Let's see who we're dealing with, then," Ebrill said, and cast a reveal spell. The dark dress faded first, the woman's body exposed but burning bright with flames in places until that, too, flew away. Darkness lifted like a veil, revealing the dark form of a kneeling woman.

"Irla?" Ebrill gasped while taking a step back, voice nearly cracking. "No... how?"

"You were turned to stone," Kordelia added. "One of us."

With a shake of her head, Irla laughed and moved her hands quickly, creating a spell that held us each in place. "I was never truly one of you, was I?"

"Of course, you were," Ebrill countered.

"Your kind always looked down on my people." Irla stepped into the light and more of the puzzle came together—her dark skin, white hair. This wasn't the Irla I had met in the mountains back in time. This version of her, which I had to assume was the real one, was a Drow.

"We were allies with the Drow," Kordelia argued.

"You treated my people like slaves," Irla spat back. "How can you talk to me about allies?"

"It wasn't like that," Kordelia pleaded. Seeing someone as tall and intimidating as her plead gave the conversation a whole new meaning. It made me wonder what had really gone on between these two groups so long ago.

"You see it your way, I see it mine," Irla mumbled. "Now… it ends."

She lunged for the gargoyle, a blade of flames appearing in her hands, and I could tell that Kordelia wasn't even going to fight her—just let it happen. I couldn't allow that, though, so I stepped in to meet that blade with my ice-forged one.

Only, at the last second Irla let her blade fade, so that instead of our blades meeting, mine sank deep into her chest. It didn't draw blood, but instantly began to make her freeze over as it had with the rocky skin or armor of the giant.

She was held there momentarily, looking at me with a sense of relief and satisfaction, and then fell apart, shattering on the ground. It had been as if she wanted the release, and that troubled me.

Level up. Sweet.

***Level 7 MAGE***

***Statistics***
***Strength: 22***
***Defense: 17***
***Speed: 19***

***Luck: 15***
***Charisma: 15***

***Mana: 600***

***Recent Spells***
***Gorffwys (sleep); Frost Footing; Ice Wall; Ice Claw; Frost Bite; Flurries***

THE NEW LEVEL almost felt wrong, confusing. But… flurries? I'd take that, whatever it meant. For now, we still had Fatiha to deal with.

# 27

Fatiha stood in the corner, face pale and eyes wide with worry. I moved for her and she seemed like she was about to fight, but instead held up both hands.

"You win," Fatiha said. "For now. But when she—"

"Give me the tree," I interrupted.

She clenched her teeth, glaring. Her hand shook as she indicated the far wall. Moving up to it, the wall gave way —the same wall I'd made an escape through during the fight with Irla! One more foot, maybe, and I would have found it. Unless there was some other magic to the hiding part that I wasn't aware of.

The tree floated out to her, and she turned, letting it go to me.

"The Nine are out there, waiting…" she said. "When you meet Thiten in person, the real Thiten, you will die."

"We'll take our chances," I said, frowning and mulling over the tree.

"How do we make it work?" Kordelia asked.

I had the answer, I hoped. Pricking my finger on the tree as I had seen Fatiha do, I let my blood drip into place, then willed my aunt to return.

"Come on," I muttered.

When it didn't respond, Ebrill stepped up next to me, hand on my arm, and arched an eyebrow. I knew immediately what she was thinking. Transmutation to make it respond to me. No sooner did the thought hit me than the tree started to glow as the blood changed, and the form of my aunt appeared.

"Hello, Jericho." She stood before me, seemingly the real her—not even transparent as before.

"Aunt Gertrude," I said, unable to believe she was standing there before me.

She glanced around, clenched her jaw, and moved close, her voice low. "This doesn't look good."

"We're in the enemy's hideout so, no, it's not. We need to open the Liahona."

My aunt turned to Ebrill, then Kordelia.

"It's time," Kordelia said with a reassuring nod. "He brought us back. He can find the others. Defeat the evil that once tried to take the power for itself."

"Such faith in him, and… me."

"Don't tell me you're betraying us, too," I said.

Gertrude turned to me, very solemn. "Never." Another moment, and she added, "So, you're ready?"

"The forces of darkness are upon us," Kordelia cut in. "We have no choice."

"Jericho," Gertrude stared, eyes never leaving me, "are *you* ready?"

"I am," I replied.

"Very well. It's a simple spell, really. Hold the Liahona and repeat after me."

I did, and then together we chanted a long spell. As each word was muttered, small wisps of magical light escaped the Liahona, circling us, until at the end it was a burst of lights so that we saw nothing else but that magic and each other.

"Good luck," Gertrude said, fading into the light.

"You can't leave us," I said, a sudden anxiety taking over me at the sight of her going.

"I have no choice," she replied, hand up in farewell. "I am the last of the spell—the final piece of the key."

"Thank you," I managed, watching as the last of her faded.

When she was gone, the light burst outward, causing us to shield our faces. Sensing that it was over, I looked, and then stared around us in amazement. What I saw wasn't that rocky area beneath the Virginia soil, but a land of green waters receding from its borders, a bridge of light connecting it to a land far off. Avalon was reconnecting with our world.

More than the awe I felt at seeing this, though, was the immense power I sensed at my fingertips. Maybe it wouldn't all be mine, or fully accessible, but it was there, and eventually I could learn how to harness it. The breeze from Avalon touched my cheek, warm and comforting. It pulled me into this land of magic and made me never want to leave.

And, there was something there. A figure, rising from a point in the distance, that turned to face us, smiling. I recognized her from my dreams—Rianne.

"The magic has been restored," she said, voice carrying

as if she were right next to us. “But the war has just begun.”

“I understand,” I said, nodding in a deferential bow. “We will do what is needed.”

“I have no doubts.”

Laughter sounded, distant but all too familiar. I turned to Ebrill, who was clearly aware of it as well.

“Fatiha,” Kordelia said, confirming my thought. She turned to Rianne. “And the others? Aerona?”

“Aerona will join you, shortly,” Rianne replied. “But I must stay here. The others are gone.”

“As in…?” I asked, horrified.

“Not dead. But… gone. As Gertrude managed to find Ebrill and Kordelia,” she paused to smile at each, “some of the others have been discovered. You may find them, wake them, and bring them to your side. However…”

“Irla?” Ebrill asked. “We are aware of her betrayal, and she has been dealt with.”

Rianne took the news with a mixture of relief and sorrow, nodding. “She may not be the only one you find that darkness has corrupted. Be careful out there. For now, go back to your business. I will be here, accessible, helping you along your journey.”

“Thank you,” I said as the light faded and we were pulled back to our underground room.

At first, I thought my eyes were playing tricks on me, but then I realized it was simply them adjusting to the darkness. And it wasn’t simply the darkness of the room, but dark, swirling shadows moving around Fatiha as she moved her hands, chanting.

“She wanted us to have the tree,” Steph said, voice full of awe. “Giving us our power, in exchange for hers.”

It made sense, in a twisted way. If she believed she could work to get the Nine Ladies back, to have the power to take us down even if we had access to Avalon, her move could work. Let us have our power, in exchange for hers.

Or maybe she was so twisted that she didn't care what happened to the world, as long as she got hers.

Her dark eyes rose to mine, her cackling laughter echoing all around as she held up a hand, eyeing me as if about to cast a spell.

My hands rose, too, suddenly shaking at the amount of power I felt in them. So much power, ready to be cast upon her. Those dark eyes moved to my hands, her laughter and even her smile fading.

"Not today, then," she said, and then waved her hands in a circle around herself so that the shadows swept up in a spiral that engulfed her, and then she was gone.

Teleported, I supposed.

A moment later, a flash of light appeared through the roof and then stone and earth crashed down, followed by a solid figure that landed with a thud, wings tucked back behind her head, ready for a fight. I instantly recognized her as Aerona.

She stood, looking exhausted but ready for a fight.

No words. The three gargoyles embraced, holding each other for a long beat, and then they charged back the way we came.

"That's… Aerona?" Steph asked.

"Yup."

"Not very talkative, I guess." Steph frowned. "Like, where's the 'it's been so long, how're you doing?' or any of that? Doesn't even need a battle briefing. Shows up and just charges out?"

"I think maybe she shares a mental connection with one or both of the other two? I'm not sure, but—"

Shisa let out a whimper, interrupting us.

"How about instead of talking, you two hurry your asses!" Kordelia shouted back. "We have to get out of here by sunrise!"

Damn, she was right. And judging by the flashing red and blue I saw through the hole Aerona made when she arrived, there was a situation above that would be better avoided. So, we ran, Shisa taking the lead while my mind attempted to come to grips with the idea that my aunt was actually gone, and that our team hadn't only grown by one more, but that we were going to keep growing.

We had a team to find, Fatiha and the Nine—or some of the Nine, anyway—to hunt down, and an army of evil to stop.

I couldn't wait.

# 28

Where else could we have gone, other than the mansion? It needed fixing up, sure, and safeguards to ensure that whatever evil Fatiha had done was counteracted, but we had the magic of Avalon. We had my team, which now included Aerona, and I better understood Shisa now.

According to Ebrill's guess, we still had about an hour until sunrise. I set about redecorating the house in terms of my transmutation abilities, while the ladies put up every sort of defensive ward they could think of. I searched deep, connecting to the house and surrounding grounds, ensuring no passages or other secrets were left by Fatiha, looking for anything that could be used against us. Several passages led out from under the house, but I closed those off until a time when we might be able to use them to our advantage. As I finished, I briefly checked into the news on Steph's phone—the only one among us, and only source in the house. Apparently, Virginia had suffered minor earthquakes that had resulted in fires.

How strange, to know the truth when everyone else was being lied to.

All in all, the defenses didn't take long, and soon I went to find the others, discovering that they had taken over the master bedroom. My aunt had kept it sparse but pristine.

Aerona and Kordelia were talking with Steph, filling Aerona in on everything they could, while Shisa sat at the window, always on guard. Seeing Aerona in the light of the house and in her gargoyle form, I was struck by the difference between her and the other two. While Ebrill and Kordelia had both been a sort of blue and purple shade, Aerona's skin was almost gold, eyes light blue in a way that reminded me of a pendant my mother used to wear. This gargoyle was every bit as beautiful as the other two, and Steph. Even with her frame slightly smaller than the other two, and with horns that curved around instead of flowing back, she had an aura about her that spoke of power. Knowing who she had been in the past, the aura made complete sense.

"Wards in place?" I asked.

Kordelia nodded. "We washed up, too. You might want to, when Ebrill's done."

I glanced down and saw what she meant. Our fighting and underground travels had left me filthy.

"What's next?" I asked. "I mean, can I do something while you all are… stone?"

"We," Steph corrected me. "Can we do something?"

"Right."

Kordelia scrunched her nose in thought and turned to Aerona.

"I have a lead," Aerona said. "It has to do with Avalon

and, well, I'm trying to put the pieces together still, but think we'll have something to go off. Tomorrow night, we'll begin."

"And if the enemy attacks during the day?" Steph asked. "Or even tomorrow night?"

"Let them try," I replied, puffing out my chest. "We'll be fucking ready for them."

"So, it's true?" Aerona asked. "You're the one, now?"

"The one?"

"You know. The wielder of the Liahona. Our clan's leader, in a sense."

I considered this, at first about to be humble, to deny it. But you know what? Fuck it, I loved the idea of being the leader of this group, so I nodded. "That's right."

Kordelia grinned, apparently liking this confident side of me.

"Well, then," Aerona said, eyeing me up and down. "I look forward to fighting under your command."

"She looks forward to doing a lot more than fighting under you," Kordelia said with a chuckle.

Aerona eyed her, allowed a laugh, then turned back to me, very matter-of-factly. "She's not wrong. But... not yet. I'd like to see this city of ours, this land of the future where magic is thought to be myth." As she went to the doorway, she nodded to Steph. "It's a pleasure to meet you."

"You, too."

As soon as she was gone, Ebrill emerged from the bathroom, completely nude. Her hair was wet and hanging over her shoulders, a droplet of water falling between her perfect breasts. She stood in the doorway and beckoned me in. "We don't have much time before sunrise, and… I'd like to take full advantage of it. Hurry, now. Rinse."

"Excuse me?" I turned from her to Steph, who was already grinning and pulling off her shirt.

"You heard the woman," Steph said. "Get your ass naked and in the water."

Staring at her perky little breasts and then back to Ebrill with her muscular frame and curves, I felt myself stiffening downstairs and knew that, as exhausted as I was, there was no way I was too exhausted for this.

"I'll let you three get to it," Kordelia said, heading for the door with a humored glance at my exposed bulge.

"Join us," Steph said.

Kordelia paused and assessed her, then Ebrill. "I'm… not ready, yet."

"Well, when you are, you know where to find us." Steph blew her a kiss, giggled, and then took my hand to lead me into the bathroom. There, she started undressing me by pulling up my shirt and kissing me in the process. Other hands found my belt and I turned my head to see Ebrill, who kissed me, too. She then lowered and kissed my back as she pulled my pants off, then the boxer briefs, so that I stood there, naked.

I stepped into the water, very aware of them both watching.

"Lean back, on this side," Steph motioned.

It was a large, whirlpool-style bath. When I was relaxing against the side toward them as instructed, they started cleaning me, hands in the water and making sure to get every inch of me. *Every* inch.

Steph pulled me out as Ebrill sat on the edge of the tub, taking me and allowing me to kiss her lips, then her neck as my hands massaged her breasts. One hand ran along her side, grabbed her ass, and then worked its way over to find her wet pussy. Her wings flapped as my fingers found their way into her opening, a reaction I wasn't used to, but then she was kissing me fervently as her hand stroked my erect cock.

Steph stepped up behind us, hands between my legs to fondle my balls. She ran one hand along my ass, even moving her fingers to tickle my hole. I wasn't sure about that, as it felt good but too ticklish, so I laughed but moved her hand aside. She pulled me into a kiss as Ebrill knelt and ran her tongue along the base of my cock.

My hand went to her head, the other caressing Steph. Before I knew it, as Ebrill started bobbing up and down on my cock, my fingers were caressing horn. Her long, hard horns. A strange thought, but the action caused her to moan and get even more into it, bobbing up and down while stroking and moaning.

Finally, she couldn't take it and pushed me away and into Steph, who leaned back against the tub, grabbed my cock and lifted one leg to make room for it. I slid in, feeling Ebrill now at my ass. Not her hand, but her face, buried in there, tongue tickling my ass. Only, this time it didn't tickle, but felt damn good. She did this for a moment as I gently moved with Steph, then sat up and fingered herself while watching as my thrusts increased with passion-fueled intensity.

If there had been any doubt on Kordelia's or Aerona's parts about what we were doing, there wasn't now. Steph was pounding her fist against the side of the tub, moaning and occasionally yelping, while Ebrill licked her lips, breathing heavily.

Then Steph pushed me back so that I slid out. She motioned to the bed and we moved over, Ebrill following. Steph pushed me back, climbed on, and slid onto my cock. It couldn't have been more than three or four thrusts before she collapsed on me, body tense as her orgasm took hold.

"Fuck me, Jay!" she shouted, then let out a lower, more sensual, "fuckkk… me."

She was done, moving aside and lying there like she was about to pass out while Ebrill rolled me over on top of her. Wings spread and head up so that her horns wouldn't puncture the pillow, it wasn't the most natural of positions, but she seemed fine so I slid in, happy to oblige.

"Show me how a leader fucks," she said. "I want the full power of Avalon rocking my world."

I blinked, taken back by that, and she laughed.

"Oh, just fuck me already," she added, pulling me in and thrusting her hips with the motion. My cock fully in her, all of my muscles clenched at once, then slowly let loose as I started moving, the two of us like one. I felt her around the entirety of my shaft, enjoyed the sensation of my balls against her warm legs, and grabbed her under the shoulders to get leverage.

Soon, she was gripping me, claws in my shoulders in a painful, yet oddly pleasurable, way. Moaning, clenching, smiling.

As Ebrill climaxed, a creak sounded from the door. It was open. Kordelia watched, biting her lip. Steph motioned her in, and, to my surprise, the large gargoyle entered. She approached, hand running along her exposed stomach, up to the curve of the armor that covered her breasts, and then up to the side of her neck, where it lingered as she leaned in to my ear.

I lay there, not sure what to expect as Ebrill's tight pussy tensed around my cock, her heavy breathing telling me she was still experiencing the pleasure of her climax.

Kordelia's lips almost touched my ear as she whispered into it, "I'm about to get so hard right now."

"What?" I said, turning to her in confusion.

Her eyes showed her desire to laugh as she pointed past me to the window. "Hard as stone."

Sure enough, sunrise would be there any second. Already the sky was light blue, a hint of yellow at the edges.

"Shit," I said, quickly sliding my cock out of Ebrill and moving off her. One last moan from her, and then she was stone—frozen until the next night, lying there with legs spread in the act of an orgasmic aftershock.

It almost made me laugh, but more so, was hot as fuck.

Steph eyed me, shrugged, and beckoned me over. "I want you to finish in my mouth."

I couldn't argue with that.

She led me back into the bathroom, knelt at the side of the tub, and cupped water with her hand. Using this water, she briefly washed my cock, then used her wet hands to massage my balls as she took me in her mouth, moving her head up and down. Soon, her hands were working me, too, and when I came in her mouth, all of the fighting and darkness and negative bullshit was washed away. All that mattered in that moment was the look of adoration in her eyes, the sexy way she took my cock from her mouth and flicked her tongue along the tip, and the tingling sensation through my body as she ran the fingers of her other hand up along my abs.

"I missed you," she said. "Even if I didn't really know you—or the real me didn't—I missed you."

I laughed, pulled her up and gently kissed her. "It's good to have the real you here, with me."

"And not because I just swallowed your cum?"

"No, although that's a nice bit of icing on the cake."

She laughed, kissed me again, and then led me back to the bed. We paused there, looking at Ebrill's nude, stone form. I nodded to the next room over, and then noticed Shisa eyeing us.

"You got this?" I asked.

Shisa nodded and turned back to the window.

This time, I led Steph. Soon, we were in bed in the guest room, her curled up in my arms, both of us drifting off to sleep. We had adventures ahead of us, more power than I could've ever imagined, and my cock was throbbing with blissful memories of what we had just done.

I was in heaven.

***THE END***

# ABOUT THE AUTHOR

**Jamie Hawke**

After working on Marvel properties and traveling the world, Jamie Hawke decided to settle down and write fun, quirky, and sexy pulp science fiction and superhero books. Are they all harem? Oh yeah. Oh yeahhhh.

It all started when Jamie was eleven, creating nude superhero comics with his best friend. What perverts! But hey, they were fun and provided good fodder for jokes up into their adult years. Now the stories have evolved, but they capture that same level of fun. Hopefully you will enjoy them as much as the author loved writing them!

https://www.facebook.com/JamieHawkeAuthor

# READ NEXT

Thank you for reading! Please consider leaving reviews on Amazon and Goodreads. And don't miss out on the NEXT RELEASE by signing up for the newsletter:

**SIGN UP HERE**

* * *

You can now get Ex Gods and Psychobitches (both in the Supers universe). Enjoy!

A Marine in space, three hot super ladies, and an army of supervillains out to get them. What could go wrong?

* * *

I am the law! Well, kinda. More like a bounty hunter, but I

still put a foot up the @$$ of injustice and bring criminals down.

***

Did you see the references to Planet Kill in the book and wonder what that was? It's not a real planet that I know of, but it is a real book! You can grab book one and two on Amazon!

Grab PLANET KILL now!

**Form your harem. Kill or be killed. Level up and loot. Welcome to Planet Kill.**

* * *

## MY OTHER WORKS: JUSTIN SLOAN

You also might want to read the stuff I write that isn't

harem/ spicy sauce stuff. If so, you'll want to head over to the Justin Sloan books. Here they are!

**Books by Justin Sloan**

**SCIENCE FICTION**

**ASCENSION GATE (Space Opera with Dragon Shifters and Vampires)**
**Star Forged**
**(More coming soon!)**

**BIOTECH WARS (Space Station Genetic Engineering)**
**Project Destiny ($0.99)**
**Project Exodus**
**Project Ascent**

**VALERIE'S ELITES (Vampires in Space - Kurtherian Gambit Universe 4 Book Series)**
**Valerie's Elites**
**Death Defied**
**Prime Enforcer**
**Justice Earned**

**RECLAIMING HONOR (Vampires and Werewolves - Kurtherian Gambit Universe 8 Book Series, Complete)**
**Justice is Calling**
**Claimed by Honor**
**Judgment has Fallen**
**Angel of Reckoning**
**Born into Flames**
**Defending the Lost**

Return of Victory

**Shadow Corps (Space Opera Fantasy/ Light LitRPG - Seppukarian Universe 3 Book Series, Complete)**

Shadow Corps
Shadow Worlds
Shadow Fleet
Shadow Mystic

**War Wolves (Space Opera Fantasy - Seppukarian Universe 3 Book Series, Complete)**

Bring the Thunder
Click Click Boom
Light Em Up

**Syndicate Wars (Space Marines and Time Travel - Seppukarian Universe 5 Book Series, Complete)**

First Strike
The Resistance
Fault Line
False Dawn
Empire Rising

## FANTASY

**The Hidden Magic Chronicles (Epic Fantasy - Kurtherian Gambit Universe 4 Book Series, Complete)**

Shades of Light
Shades of Dark
Shades of Glory
Shades of Justice

**FALLS OF REDEMPTION (Epic Fantasy Series 4 Book Series)**

**Land of Gods (NOW FREE!)**

**Retribution Calls**

**Tears of Devotion**

**MODERN NECROMANCY (Supernatural Thriller 3 Book Series, Complete)**

**Death Marked**

**Death Bound**

**Death Crowned**

**CURSED NIGHT**

**Hounds of God**

Made in the USA
Las Vegas, NV
03 May 2021